VHAIDRA & THE DRAGON OF TEMPLE MOUNT

NICHOLAS STANOSHECK

INDIA · SINGAPORE · MALAYSIA

Notion Press

No.8, 3rd Cross Street,
CIT Colony, Mylapore,
Chennai, Tamil Nadu – 600004

First Published by Notion Press 2021
Copyright © Nicholas Stanosheck 2021
All Rights Reserved.

ISBN 978-1-7349140-2-3

This a work of fiction. Names, characters, businesses,
places, events, locales, and incidents are either the products of the author's
imagination or used in a fictitious manner.
Any resemblance to actual persons, living or dead,
or actual events is purely coincidental.

E-Book Edition ISBN: 978-1-7349140-3-0

Library of Congress Control Number: 2020919836

LCCN Imprint Name: Dallas, Texas

Publisher: Notion Press

Cover Design: Stan Saint Yak

Editor: Obed Joshua

The following Adobe Fonts are licensed for personal & commercial use and
were used in this publication:

IM Fell Great Primer © Igino Marini, IM Fell

Modesto Condensed © Jim Parkinson, Parkinson Type Design

DEDICATION

To Lakshman Naidu

Ramu Ganapath Velu,
whose business decisions led me to becoming a
Lean Six Sigma Black Belt
and indirectly led me to pivot,
to become a top-selling, full-time writer.

CONTENTS

This book is written and edited in British English.

FOREWORD

First, I would like to express my thanks to the author, Nicholas Stanosheck, for giving me this opportunity to write this foreword. This is the second book in the series, which I have edited. And while working on the two books, Nik and I, have developed a mutually beneficial professional relationship, which helped me to become a better editor.

To introduce this book to you, readers, I thought really long and hard about what to reveal and what not to. Then, I decided, as I should, to draw parallels with this incredible work of fantasy fiction with the real world that we live in. Nik, as an author, is incredibly skilled at writing fantasy fiction that is highly relevant to the present day. The experience the author has gained through the various roles he had taken professionally in his life have enriched the book immensely.

The first interesting parallel that I would like the readers to know is about xenophobia and hate crimes, fueled by the fear spread by populism, which is increasingly on the rise around the world. The book serves as a tool to highlight the importance of tolerance and the benefits of harmony in the way in which everyone could understand. The way Nik has built this incredible moral into the series is highly commendable.

The second parallel is the relevance of religion. 'The Way' described in the books resembles many of the monotheistic religions around the world. While the religion adds a special dimension to Nik's fantasy world, the author also does not shy away from pointing out the many flaws in the people of The Way, and how, through love alone, can people be brought closer to God.

Finally, Nik's writing skills are spectacular, and I believe that it would keep the readers hooked until the last page. This is was evident even in his first novel, *Vhaidra and The Destiny of Nikodemos*, and if anything, his skills have only gotten better in this book. The book, while being incredibly enjoyable for hardcore fantasy readers, it makes a great children's book and is fascinating for the video-game oriented teenagers of today. This, I believe, is the author's greatest strength – to write literature that is relevant and enjoyable for every reader.

– Obed Joshua

THE END OF ONE STORY IS JUST THE BEGINNING OF ANOTHER

"**D**on't worry, Hypo, I am fully educated in the ways of *marital relations,* as you call them here in the overworld," Vhaidra boldly stated to her new husband.

Hypodiakonos Nikodemos replied, "How? I thought you were a..."

"I am, but young *drow* females are allowed to watch their mother matron and taught how to use mating activity for both pleasure of oneself, and either the pleasure or destruction of their mate," the dark elf explained.

"Destruction by mating?" Hypo excitedly asked, "I thought only *succubi* did this?"

The drow monk explained, "Succubi use mating to get a male to submit his eternal soul. Drow can use mating as a way to physically destroy a mate of prey."

"Mate of prey?" the human cleric asked his wife.

"Don't worry, Hypo. You are not my prey," she grinned slyly.

Hypo frowned, "I am sorry to say that I am not educated in the ways of marital relations, my dear."

"Don't worry, Hypo. I will teach you!"

"That's what the succubi say!" he teased her.

"What?" she exclaimed loudly.

"Never mind, dear," he said, winking at his new wife.

With that being said, she pushed him down in their marital bed and gave him a night he would never forget – a night he would also limp away from, as drow sensuality and human sensuality were not perfectly in line with one another. One of the many lessons that he learned that night.

But what happened next was a lesson that he never expected or planned for...

CHAPTER I
AFTER THE APOCALYPSE

YEAR 1

Whe n *Miriam* returned to the *Orphanage* of the *Transfiguration Cenobium* after the *Battle for Sicyon* against the *Jet Fist Cult*, she found that she could no longer be a milkmaid. During the battle, she had died and was resurrected by *Elder Dionysios*. When she was resurrected, she returned as a sixteen-year-old young lady. Try as much as he could, *Mikhail* could not draw milk from her much smaller, now milk-less breasts any longer.

Miriam, having already lost her family to the Jet Fist Cult, and now also losing her mission of being a milkmaid, was devastated. She had almost felt like an adopted mother to Mikhail, having nursed him ever since she met him, Elder Dionysios the half-orc, Hypodiakonos Nikodemos, the only human of their group, Vhaidra the drow elf, and *Ti'erra*, the gold wood dwelf in *Halab*.

She started to wonder if meeting this group had been a blessing, as it seemed at first, or if this was truly a curse. Simply choosing to be a travelling milkmaid for hire had gotten her parents and husband killed, and then, eventually, herself. Even though she had been resurrected, part of her felt dead, as she had lost her what she had thought was her new mission in life.

This was a mission that she had taken up immediately after she found that she was unable to bring a live baby to term. Although her baby had died, her breasts were still full of milk. So, this ability had given her some solace. Being able to give other babies life-giving nutrition, even if she could not have babies of her own, was her destiny, she had thought.

Even though she was happy to have previously been able to provide for the baby that the party had with them, she had to admit that she looked at Mikhail differently since she learned that he was a half-dragon and not a pure human. She still cared for him, nonetheless.

Questioning what to do with her life, she visited Elder Dionysios in the catacomb hermitage and asked for his advice.

"Miriam, you are the nouna to Vhaidra now. While you are physically much younger than her, you are older than her in The Way. You must teach her how to act as a wife of a Hypodiakonos of The Ancient of Days," Elder Dionysios continued, "Even though you no longer can be a milkmaid to Mikhail, he has grown attached to you. So, I think you should visit him every day. He is used to being with you first thing in the morning and many times throughout the day until he goes to sleep at night. The best way to do this is to continue working at the Orphanage of the Transfiguration Cenobium. However, instead of working as a milkmaid, perhaps, you could do our God's work as a monk."

Miriam was surprised at this advice and told Elder Dionysios that she would consider it and speak with *Archimandrite Olga,* the head monastic of the Orphanage of the Transfiguration Cenobium, about this idea. If she decided to follow his advice, it would be a total change as she had been happily married before her husband's death at the hands of the Jet Fist Cult, and she had only become a milkmaid once she lost her child at birth. She had never considered the monastic life, but she did as she promised the elder and spoke with Archimandrite Olga about this.

Archimandrite Olga was very convincing, "Miriam, everything happens for a reason. I believe that Elder Dionysios is correct about your destiny. You are a devout girl, you have sacrificed to help others, and have been resurrected by The Ancient of Days. Surely, this is the least that you can do for him. Consider it for one full year, visiting your *vaptistiki*, this *dark elf* that you are nouna for, and guide her in The Way. Once she becomes a mother, she will be terribly busy, and she will not have as much time for you to teach her. After this occurs, this would be an ideal time for you to join the monastery if you wish to follow the Creator-Logos-Ghost's will."

⸻ ❦ ⸻

Archon Justinian of Sicyon had given Hypodiakonos Nikodemos one of his homes, *Omorfia Dipla Sto Potami* on the edge of Sicyon, near the main city gate. He had granted him this home in exchange for the land that Nikodemos owned, as the Jet Fist Cult had destroyed the hypodiakonos' home on that land. The archon had the rubble removed from the land and started building what he called a *Noskomeio*, a place to heal the sick and dying of Sicyon. After the massive amounts of people injured and killed in the

Battle for Sicyon, he felt called to create this for his city.

When the cornerstone was set in place, Episkopos Chrysostom came and blessed the building of the Noskomeio, saying,

"O Ancient of Days, Who made the Ten Heavens with wisdom and has established the earth upon its sure foundations, the Creator and Author of all living things, look upon these Your servant, Archon Justinian, to whom it has seemed good to set up a house of healing in the dominion of Your Power, and to rear it by building; establish it upon a stable rock, and found it according to Your divine word in the Books of Preparedness so that neither wind, nor flood, nor any other thing shall be able to harm it; graciously grant that they may bring it to completion, and deliver all them who shall wish to dwell therein from every attack of the enemy; for Yours is the dominion, and Yours is the Kingdom, and the Power, and the Glory, of the Creator-Logos-Ghost, both now and ever, and to the ages of ages. Amin."

The home that now belonged to the hypodiakonos was currently inhabited by Nikodemos, Vhaidra, and in one of the guest rooms, Ti'erra the dwelf dancer. At first, the Cleric thought that Elder Dionysios would live with them too, but his spiritual guide had said that this would not be necessary since his catacomb hermitage was so close by.

The Elder, while he enjoyed the time with his friends, also enjoyed the time in deep prayer alone and undistracted as a hermit. That said, he often visited the couple, since he was the guardian of the internalised armour within the hypodiakonos. He also had become the spiritual guide for the newly wedded couple, although Miriam was supplementing that role for her vaptistiki, the dark elf Vhaidra.

At Nikodemos' urging, the Elder used his abilities to create a secret passage from the catacomb hermitage to the estate of Omorfia Dipla Sto Potami. Any of its inhabitants only had to turn a giant ship's wheel that was decorated with a carving of three angels: a seraph, a cherub, and an ophan. The wheel was mounted to the wall, and then, a hidden passageway would open connecting the two very different residences.

———— ⋯•◆•⋯ ————

Ti'erra knew that the monk and the cleric had been exceedingly kind to her, letting her stay in their gorgeous home, but she knew that she should not stay there forever, especially if they started to have children. Even though Vhaidra, the dark elf monk, was her best friend and she loved spending time with her, she had a desire to be self-sufficient and have true privacy when she so desired. She hadn't had that since before she went to work at *Brother*, the tavern of the Jet Fist Gang and Cult that they had called a 'club,' because it was where they met and planned their attacks.

Ti'erra did like having access to Elder Dionysios, and often, used the wheel of an angelic trinity to go ask him mundane questions, as she enjoyed spending time with the wizard. While these interruptions often annoyed the half-orc Elder, he tolerated her and treated her with kindness always, which just strengthened Ti'erra's unrequited feelings for him.

During one of these visits, Ti'erra mentioned her desire to be independent.

Dionysios suggested to her, "Maybe, Miriam will need a roommate if she desires to not be a constant guest at the monastery. Then, you can get a house with her."

He then suggested that the dwelf seek out the human ranger and ask her.

———•◦●◦•———

Miriam wasn't exactly thrilled about the idea of sharing a home with Ti'erra, but she did not know many people in Sicyon, and she needed a somewhat stable place to stay while considering joining the cenobitic life. To make a truly unbiased decision, she needed to stay in a place other than the monastery, where she has been staying as a guest. So, Miriam hesitantly agreed with the dwelf's suggestion once she found out that was inspired by the Elder.

"Oh, Ranger, we will have the best times! But don't worry. I know it is important to have privacy as well. Just let me know when you need private time alone or with anyone else."

"Ti'erra, I plan on visiting with the Iroas family since I am Vhaidra's nouna. I also volunteer at the Orphanage of the Transfiguration Cenobium. When I get home from those places, I will definitely want a quiet time alone. What will you be doing all day?"

"Well, I used to work at the tavern, *Brother*, before it was destroyed. So, I am looking at working at the *Pink Dragon Tavern*."

"Oh, what kind of work will you be doing? Being a barmaid?" Miriam asked, rolling her eyes and hoping that she was wrong.

"Oh, no, I am a dancer, not a bar wench. I will dance for money."

If Miriam disliked the idea of Ti'erra being a barmaid, she liked the idea of her being a dancer even less. The two were really like oil and water, a very odd set of roommates. Miriam was a very devout human follower of The Way, while Ti'erra was a very ecumenical dwelf, and prayed to whatever god or goddess that those around her prayed to. Miriam did not like that about the half-elf half-dwarf but thought that maybe, she could use it to her advantage and get Ti'erra to join her in morning and evening prayers each day. By doing so, perhaps, she could then convince the dwelf that the Creator-Logos-Ghost was the only god that she should pray to. After all, if Elder Dionysios could convert a drow, of all races, to

The Way, maybe she could convert this dwelf, a *half sylvan* and *half gold dwarf* to The Way as well.

It would be a challenge, as she knew that many elves generally had a very carefree way of life, and few, outside the dark elves and clergy of the high and wood elves, were devout to their gods and goddesses. It was quite different from humans, who, in her experience, tended to be more devout in their worship to their one chosen god or goddess. What Miriam did not know was that dwarves tended to be very devout followers of their deities. Unfortunately for her, Ti'erra had taken up the elvish trait of carefree religious life from her half-elf side, rather than the zeal of her half-dwarven ancestry.

"Ti'erra, if we are to be roommates, I do ask that we say our prayers together. Every morning, every night, and mealtime prayers when we are together."

"Of course, Ranger. I always joined in the communal prayer of the wizard and the cleric ever since they rescued me from the Jet Fist Cult. I've grown accustomed to them."

"I'm glad to hear that," Miriam replied, cracking a little smile at last.

CHAPTER II
PREGNANT PAUSE

At night, Nikodemos liked to hold his wife, Vhaidra, close to him, placing his chest to her forehead, so he could kiss her when she looked up into his blue eyes.

One night, she asked why he preferred this position. "Hypo, the first time you held me, my back was to your chest and you draped an arm over me, but now, you like to hold me the other way. Why?"

"Well, dear, as much as I would like to say otherwise, the first time was not intentional. You had your back to me while you watched for danger and protected me since I was injured. During the night, my arm slipped from my hip to your chest."

"I'll always remember that night. I was shocked at how much heat you radiated, and it was nice to be able to stay warm. I allowed myself to feel protected by a male for the first time ever, with your arm over me."

"I love that thought too, but now, we are not in danger in our own bed each night, and I like to be able to look into your beautiful eyes, kiss your delicious lips, and nibble on the points of your ears."

A shudder went through Vhaidra's body as she purred, "Oh, how I love it when you do that! I'm not sure how you figured out how much I like you to do that, but please never stop doing that!"

Nikodemos smiled, laughed, and once again, began to gently kiss and then nibble on her ears, which drove Vhaidra crazy with desire.

As had happened in the past when he did this, he awoke the next day sore, but happy.

———•◦●◦•———

As Miriam had predicted, Vhaidra had quickly become pregnant after her marriage. Miriam figured she only had seven or so months of teaching Vhaidra about The Way after she found out about the pregnancy. Vhaidra let Miriam know that she was actually quite wrong about that.

Drow, like all elves, had a gestation period of twenty-four months, not nine months like humans. Miriam had never heard of this and stayed around when the midwife, Valeria, was making her first prenatal checkup to make sure that this was true.

The midwife that Hypodiakonos Nikodemos had hired had explained to them that a *half-elf* or *half-human* baby, as *elves* called them, would gestate for about one year or twelve months and that this could be painful for Vhaidra since her body was not made for such a large baby, especially one that would grow that fast.

Some female elves were even known to die during childbirth when pregnant with the child of a much larger human father. Vhaidra knew that she was strong but focused even more on strengthening her abdomen muscles and doing exercises to strengthen her pelvic floor so that she could be ready for the challenge that lay ahead.

Miriam was scared for her vaptistiki and wondered if The Ancient of Days truly blessed such a dangerous union. In fact, before coming to Sicyon, she did not realise that her religion, The Way, was open to non-human races. Here, there was a half-orc, a drow, a dwelf, and even rumours of some duergars and other elves who had embraced the faith to various degrees. The temple of the Way that Miriam had attended the divine services at in *Halab* only had human congregants, monks, and clergy. She had grown up in her city that had always kept people of different faiths and races separated. One part of Halab had human followers of The Way, another part had dwarven followers of the Soulforger, and another part had the elven followers of She Who Guides. Miriam literally never knew of any other way than separation based on race and creed.

Elder Dionysios talked to Miriam about this and let her know that there were actually places in the world where the followers of The Way were all non-human races. In fact, he had heard of an all-female monastery made up exclusively of orcs, founded by a human presbyteros of The Way who had married an orc.

"Elder Dionysios, why didn't you go to one of those places after being raised in the Orphanage of the Transfiguration Cenobium?"

"Miriam, that was not the plan of The Ancient of Days. But by being a hermit in the catacombs, I was able to stay away from prying eyes, and people never knew the better. In fact, Hypodiakonos Nikodemos, when he first was appointed to take up the Armour full-time, did not even realise that I was half-orc since he was taller than me."

"How did he figure it out?"

"It was Ti'erra who let him know. Being a dwelf, she could see my face by looking up into the hood of my great schema. Since I had always kept my head down, Nikodemos had never seen my face. Before I received the Budding Rod of Harun, I had always kept my hands together under my sleeves, doing prayers on my prayer rope. He didn't seem to think anything of my muted greenish-grey feet with long yellowing nails if he had looked at them at all."

"Very interesting. I always thought that half-orcs were taller than humans since orcs are almost always much bigger than my race."

"Most half-orcs are. However, my mother was quite diminutive, I am told, and as such, I am average human height, which makes Nikodemos, who is a tall human, taller than me."

"Very interesting. Did your mother go through much pain in birthing a half-orc?" Miriam asked the half-orc.

"I am not sure. She was disgusted by me and gave me up for adoption shortly after my birth. So, I do not know any of the details of my birth."

"I am so sorry to hear this, Elder."

"Don't be. It was the will of The Ancient of Days!"

"I am worried that Vhaidra will have a hard birth. Did you know that elves normally gestate for twenty-four months? So, her baby will grow bigger and faster than her body is made for."

"I have heard. The best thing that you can do is to pray for her."

"I have been and will continue to do so, Elder."

"Very good, Miriam."

Later that day, Ti'erra brought Vhaidra a small bag of *zunjbil muskar* that she had obtained at an *apothecary* in *Rakote* before the Battle for Sicyon.

"What is this, Ti'erra?" asked the pregnant dark elf.

"It is sugared ginger, Monk."

"Get that away from me; you know I cannot stand these overworld sweetmeats!"

"I know you prefer spicy and savoury foods, but now that you are pregnant, you may find yourself craving these."

"I doubt it! I still don't understand how you overworlders can eat stuff like this!"

"I don't understand how you don't like it, Monk!"

"*Heh.* Oh, well, I'll lock them up somewhere, so I can give them back to you after I give birth."

"I won't need the empty bag. It's okay."

Vhaidra just laughed at her best friend.

"So, hey, Monk, we never have talked about it, but what made you fall in love with Nikodemos?"

"Oh, so we are talking our deepest most personal emotions now, are we, Ti'erra?"

"Well, as long as you don't mind, Monk."

"As you know, there is no such thing as love in the underworld, and so, I wasn't expecting such a thing to happen."

"That is exactly why I wondered."

"Well, even though the overworld was this mysterious patriarchy that was totally unfamiliar to me, coming from a matriarchal society, Hypo always put me first."

"How is that different from males in the underworld?"

"It was completely different. He didn't have to put me first, but he chose to put me first. That made it much more powerful to me."

"And that made you fall in love with him?"

"No, but that was the spark that started the fire. Little things like him putting his arm around me the first time we rested in a dungeon after the battle, and him feeling and smelling like a musky furnace."

"His smell and his heat?"

"It is very warm in the underworld, and so, I am often cold in the overworld at night. The heat emanating from his body gave me a sense of comfort, as did the musky smell of his sweat after a day of fighting and adventuring. I am not sure how to explain it."

"I have heard it say that everyone sweats a different smell and it only attracts a small percentage of others whom they are compatible with while offending the senses of those we are not compatible with."

"Fascinating, Ti'erra. His scent almost reminds me of a spice wagon in the underworld, but there is something different about it too."

"Hmm, I wonder what he thinks of your scent."

"Oh, he has told me. He says I smell like honeysuckles, a kind of flower here in the overworld."

"Oh, how sweet... literally!" the dwelf replied with a giggle.

"Anything else?"

"I think the fact that he knows about my culture and appreciates all races helps as well. I mean look at this group he adventures with – a dwelf dancer, a half-orc wizard, an undead ogre, and, of course, me, a dark elf monk."

"Not that he really chose us. It was more like destiny chose us to all come together."

"True, but he never rejected anyone based on their race. How many humans would treat a drow the way that he treats me?"

"Very few, I am sure."

"And it has not gained him popularity. I know some people hate him for marrying outside his race."

"So, did his zeal ever push you away? I know the Wizard is always working him about his zealousness."

"I can see how it could push him away, but his veneration of the Theotokos, the mother of The

Ancient of Days, a dark-skinned woman, really touched me in the very beginning. Much like race, he didn't treat females or males any different in deference. The fact that he believes in something so deeply and doesn't let others dissuade him, was a good feature. And now, he feels the same way about me, no matter the obstacles of overworld society. He fervently loves me for who I am, and this love is unconditional. This is something I think he has learned from The Ancient of Days."

"That is sweet. It is almost like he was made for you."

"Then, I am very blessed," Vhaidra said with a laugh.

"What's so funny about that?" Ti'erra asked.

"It is just that he always says that about me; how very blessed he is to have me as his wife, and how he thanks the Creator-Logos-Ghost for me every day."

"I am so happy for you both. I hope that one day I can be so happy in love as you both are."

"I am sure you will, my pretty dwelf friend. What male could resist being with such a happy, fun dancer like you?"

"Well, I need to go; I do not want to be late," Ti'erra replied with a giggle.

"Late for what?"

"Evening prayers. Miriam is very strict about me being back home in time to do them together."

"If you stay unmarried, she may make a monk out of you yet, Ti'erra!" Vhaidra joked with her best friend.

"Never!" replied the dwelf with a mocking sternness to her voice.

Vhaidra laughed, asked the dwelf to send greetings to Miriam, and said her goodbyes.

<hr>

After their evening prayers were completed, Miriam confided in Ti'erra that she was very worried for Vhaidra.

Ti'erra explained to the concerned Miriam about her birth, "Ranger, my mother is a *gold dwarf*, and she had no issues giving birth to me, a half-elf baby, who was bigger than the average dwarf. So, you should not be worried about the midwife's warnings. After all, dwarven gestation is generally four years, and an elf gestates for two years, so my three-year gestation was a whole year shorter than my mother would be made for. Vhaidra has got it easy compared to that!"

Learning this, Miriam became even more aware of how very different each of the so-called humanoid races was, and was shocked that crossbreeding between various races was actually successful. She also realised that while she was good at battle tactics, Ti'erra was bad at math, because her gestation of three years was only one fourth shorter than the average dwarven gestation time of four years, while Vhaidra's pregnancy would be one half the time of the normal elven gestation period. Miriam tried to explain this to Ti'erra, and the dwelf just smiled and repeated that she still thought there was nothing to worry about.

⋯●⋯

The next day, Miriam visited Archimandrite Olga, who had the opposite thought process of Ti'erra,

"Miriam, very few people knew, until recently, that Elder Dionysios was half-orc, and it was quite scandalous to some followers of The Way. I heard from some people that his small human mother, may The Ancient of Days bless her soul, actually died after giving up her freak of a son, due to the damage sustained in birthing a half-breed orc!"

"But he is a holy man who saved many lives. Surely it was the will of the Creator-Logos-Ghost that he be born?"

"I wouldn't say that his mother being raped and dying was his will at all. But The Ancient of Days can make the best of the darkness when we turn our eyes away from the things of the world and focus only on him to become *perfect saints*."

"I guess so. The Elder does not know any of the details about his birth other than that his mother was a diminutive woman. What do you know about her?"

"Unfortunately, that is all that I know about her. Such a sad story, and what a horrible way to die!" Archimandrite Olga sighed.

"We should pray for her soul then."

"Absolutely." Archimandrite Olga concurred.

The archimandrite started prayers for Elder Dionysios' mother, asking her to find eternal peace after all the troubles that she had found in her earthly life.

CHAPTER III

THE DANCE OF THE PINK WYRM

Ti'erra wanted to return to her previous occupation of being a bar dancer. So, she applied to work at the tavern called The Pink Wyrm that had replaced the place she used to work, Brother. The tavern owner, Eskandar, wanted to see her dance style. So, Ti'erra changed out of her smock and put on her giant tortoise armour that she had taken from the Shi Jin General of the North during the Battle for Sicyon. She had to have it adjusted by the local armourer and blacksmith, as it had originally been made for a taller, thinner drow as opposed to a shorter, curvier, dwelf like Ti'erra.

Ti'erra went to the middle of the tavern and placed the head of her greathammer on the floor, with the haft in the air. When it was set this way, at the top of the greathammer was a leather loop, which a larger creature could use to spin the greathammer in the air before launching it at an enemy, like Skeletogre once did to a copper dragon.

Ti'erra said to the tavern owner that in the future, he is going to want to put an indentation in the floor for her to place her hammer in. The owner was not so sure until he saw her dance.

The dwelf ran towards her greathammer and grabbed the leather loop, spinning herself around, eventually spinning ninety degrees from the haft of the weapon that she used as a dancing pole. Once she had the speed and angle she wanted. She did the splits, and after spinning that way for a minute, she placed one foot in the loop where her hand had been, while her other foot was still one hundred eighty degrees away. As she did this, she waved her hands around her chest, and these motions effectively charmed anyone watching the dance.

All the actions in of themselves were beguiling. It was Ti'erra innate sylvan magicks that entranced everyone whose eyes had caught sight of the dancer, except for an elf or another half-elf like herself, who were immune to such a spell.

After spinning like this, she slowed herself down until she was upside-down, slowly spinning as she blew kisses. Once she had come to a stop, she grabbed the haft of the greathammer near its head and then, arched herself, forming something like an uppercase letter D and then, an uppercase letter P with her body and hammer once she had pulled both of her feet to the top of her weapon.

She then seductively tossed off her armour to the tavern owner; armour that no one had seen her loosening during the first part of her dance. At this point, normally a wife might cover the eyes of her husband if they had caught sight of the disrobed half-dwarf, but even the females watching her were entranced and were unable to turn away from the display in front of them.

Ti'erra then did what seemed impossible; she pulled herself up by her feet so that she was actually standing on top of her hammer and then began to spin again, slowly using her hands to pull one of her feet up to her head, again doing the splits while she spun on her greathammer. She then bent her knee as she spun, and then, jumped into the arms of the bar owner who had set her armour down after having caught it earlier.

He gently set her down, in complete awe of what he had just seen. She grabbed her armour, held the breastplate of the armour out in front of her, and walked around while the patrons put coins in it and applauded her performance. She then transferred the coins to her bag and put her armour back on, making a huge performance of it by spinning it and herself as she danced around her greathammer. Then, Ti'erra put her weapon over her shoulder looking ready to depart The Pink Wyrm.

Ti'erra walked back over to the tavern owner and said, "It looks like I have made quite a bit of coin for doing only one short dance. It also looks like your patrons approve of my dancing skills. What say you?"

"You're hired!"

"Thanks, Tavern Owner! Now, we need to talk terms of my employment."

"Terms of your employment?" he asked, still charmed by her dance, as was everyone else in the tavern.

"Yes, I would like free meals every day, and I will only be required to dance one dance, of five minutes or less each hour, working no more than eight hours a day. I may occasionally go on long adventures, and I do not want this to affect my employment."

"That sounds fair," said Eskandar.

"Ti'erra put her bag of coins into her backpack, grabbed a contract, and handed it to the tavern owner."

"What is this?" he asked.

"A contract agreeing to what we just discussed."

"But I don't see any salary listed."

"Salary? Salary?" said Ti'erra with a laugh, "I didn't expect a salary. I simply dance for tips. Should I rewrite the contract to add a monthly salary?"

"No, no, that is okay," Eskandar speedily said, signing the contract and returning it to the dwelf.

"Thank you, Tavern Owner. I will report to work tomorrow afternoon. But since I danced today, I will take my complimentary meal of grilled boar."

"Please, call me Eskandar. I'll let the kitchen cooks know to get you your meal right away! Now, how deep of an indentation do you need for the mystical great hammer of yours?"

"Thanks, Tavern Owner. It only needs to be about two inches deep. You also might want to stain a circle around the indentation, identifying where I may be spinning, so that people know not to step in there and get kicked."

"Sure thing, Ti'erra. You are about four and a half feet tall, right?"

"Exactly," the dwelf replied with a smile.

"Good, then I will put marks five and a half feet away from the indentation on all sides. But I will also make sure that our bouncer has a good view. So, he can make sure no one goes into that marked circle or touches you."

"Oh, I can hold my own against anyone who tries, but also my hammer will make ice radiate from the indentation. So, anyone who attempts to come into the marked area is likely to slip and fall."

"Won't the ice make it dangerous for you too?"

"Nah! After all these years, I'm quite used to stepping on frozen floors, beasts, and such."

"You truly are one incredible lady, Ti'erra," Eskandar replied.

"Thank you, Tavern Owner!"

"I told you; you can call me Eskandar!"

"Thanks, but it's not my style. I never call anyone by their given names."

"You're a unique one, Ti'erra. Very unique."

Ti'erra giggled, smiled, and looked around the room. Throughout the bar, the patrons slowly started to move their eyes away from Ti'erra, and instead of watching her, began talking about her performance as the enchantment faded. While many of them thought it was the most amazing dance that they had ever seen, Ti'erra knew that it was nothing. It was only a sample of what she could do while dancing on her upside-down greathammer. They all would soon learn what all she could do.

Her friends already knew as she used many of her moves in battle when using her greathammer.

Not only would she smash it into her enemies and give them frost damage from the many enchanted aquamarines in it, but she would also look amazing doing it, distracting many of her enemies into a trance while watching her battle dance.

CHAPTER IV

SWEETMEATS ARE MADE OF THESE

ost humans did not do exercise when they were pregnant, but because her friends were always bringing her foods, spoiling her, and trying to get her to lay down and rest, Vhaidra actually increased her exercise regiment, not only working on her abdomen and pelvic floor muscles, but also her legs, arms, and back when her friends were not around.

Nikodemos joked with her, saying, "You look like you are preparing for a battle with all that added muscle that you have gained these past months!"

Vhaidra explained, "Not only am I battling all the foods brought to me in abundance, which I now inexplicitly desire to eat, but I will also be pushing something so large out of such a small space. It could definitely be seen as a battle. So, I am definitely going to be as prepared as possible."

"Strong, beautiful, and smart! Oh, how blessed I am!" her husband replied.

"Lucky man!" Vhaidra joked, grabbing his chin and kissing him, then grabbing a zunjbil muskar and sucking on it.

"What is that dear? Where did you get it?"

"They are sweetmeats that Ti'erra got in Rakote. When I feel nauseous from morning sickness, putting one of these in my mouth really helps."

"Well, if they are for medicinal purposes, then I won't ask to have one then," her husband replied with a smile, and then he added, "But, perhaps, you will allow me to kiss you so I can get a small taste of the flavour?"

"Of course, Hypo," replied his wife, giving him a quick kiss.

"Wait...does that mean that you are feeling the effects of morning sickness now?"

"No, I just was craving a sugared ginger!" she laughed.

"You? Sweets? No way!"

"I know! It is so strange, isn't it? I guess this baby wants sweets!"

"Well, you know the old saying, 'You are what you eat.' So, I guess we will be seeing a sweet Vhaidra with a sweet baby then," Hypo joked with his wife.

While Vhaidra enjoyed the reactions of her friends to her pregnancy, she didn't care for the reaction of some of the humans in Sicyon who hated her kind. It seemed her being pregnant with a half-human child only increased theses racist humans' hatred of her. In a drow city, there would be spoiling of a mother but a hidden hatred from enemies as well, just not for reasons of race, but rather, for reasons of jealousy and power.

Some of the horrible things she heard were,

"I hope your half-breed baby dies!"

"Your husband is unclean, mating with a beast like you!"

"Demos' baby is going to be so ugly, just like its mother!"

"How could a human impregnate a beast like that? What are we going to have next, half-sheep people?"

"Get out of Sicyon, you monster whore!"

"Who do you think you are, mating with a higher species?"

"Demos has dirtied himself with this disgusting creature. He deserves the demon child that she will produce!"

"'Tis disgusting when a human being mates with lower beasts. He should have killed her to cover up his indiscretion!"

In the old days, she may have chosen to kill those humans for the vile things that they said as she walked by, but as a follower of The Way and the wife of a cleric of The Way, she had to ask The Ancient of Days to help her to suppress those urges. She was also assisted by her daily exercise routines, which were an outlet for her anger and stresses.

One day, Vhaidra spoke to Elder Dionysios about this and he actually told her that this is why he had hidden his heritage, choosing to be a hermit in the catacombs, as there were a lot of people who did not like the non-human races and also warned her that her children would experience this evil as well.

"Thankfully, in The Way, the humans are not like this," she replied.

"While most are not," Elder Dionysios corrected her, "There are some followers of The Ancient of Days that are xenophobic and do not have the love of foreigners and guests, called *xenia*, in their heart yet. But please forgive them as they are also on the long path to *theosis*. The Way is not a place for perfect saints, but a spiritual hospital for sinners."

Unfortunately, Vhaidra and her children, and Nikodemos to a slightly lesser degree, would find out the truth of Elder Dionysios' words firsthand in the years to come.

CHAPTER V

THE FIRST CROW OF A MURDER

YEAR 2

"Push!" the *midwife* demanded.

Vhaidra replied to Ti'erra, "Tell the human that *I am pushing!*"

Ti'erra did as she was told, which got a smirk from Valeria, as she clearly heard Vhaidra say this.

The last eight hours of labour had been intensive. Vhaidra almost thought this baby did not want to be born! Human midwives were unique. First, she said she needed to shave Vhaidra before the baby was born. The drow did not understand her meaning until the midwife was shocked that Vhaidra had no pubic hair or leg hair. Being an elf, albeit a dark elf, she had no body hair other than the hair on her head, her eyebrows, and eyelashes. This was true of all of her race, whether female or male. She had slowly grown to appreciate humans, specifically her husband, for having hair almost everywhere. But all the same, she was glad that she had no body hair to speak of.

Ti'erra explained to her that dwarves actually had lots of hair in places other than their head, but with her being a half-elf, she had the same amount of hair as a normal human female, but shaved her legs like a dancer, since the patrons of The Pink Wyrm Tavern and of Brother before that, preferred this look.

"If I had hairy legs, I would shave them too!" Vhaidra exclaimed in disgust.

"Dwarven women are proud of their hair, Monk," The dwelf explained, "In fact, some of the gold dwarves in my home village would braid their hair in many parts of their bodies and proudly display those braids."

"What? How?"

"Well, those with the longest hairs wear armpit braids, and consider them to be decorative and help them attract a mate."

"Do they wear braids anywhere else?"

"I've seen some dwarves that have braided their arm and leg hairs and use it as a type of armour."

"Now, that is something I can understand and appreciate," the drow said with a laugh.

"There is one other place that some dwarven-kind braid hair, but the less said the better!" Ti'erra added.

Ti'erra's best friend looked at her, imagined it and decided to agree. "I may have got used to my husband's hairiness, but I don't think I could get used to the idea of body hair braids!"

The dwelf smirked for a second before Vhaidra's face contorted as she had another contraction.

"Push!" the midwife said again.

Vhaidra pushed.

Vhaidra had been pregnant for a whole year, and this baby was bigger than any drow baby would be, being a half-human, or as they called them in the *overworld,* a half-elf or half-drow. Her womb was stretched to its limit, and she knew the actual giving birth to such a large baby would be more painful than her current pain in her legs from squatting for the last eight hours, trying to push this baby out.

In the room next to her was her husband, *Hypodiakonos Nikodemos,* their spiritual guide, *Elder Dionysios,* and *Protopresbyteros Vasilios* from the local Temple of The Way. After their child was born, the presbyteros would say first day prayers for her healing and protection for Vhaidra and her baby. Prayers would again be done on the child's eighth day, where he or she would be named, receive the mysteries of *vaptisma* (ritualistic washing in holy water), *chrisma* (ritualistic anointing with holy oil), *koura* (offering the first sacrifice of hair), and his first *koinonia* for (an unknown mystery to all except full members of The Way) to become a full member of The Way. After forty days, Vhaidra could return to the *Temple of The Ancient of Days,* as she would no longer be unclean according to The Way's teachings.

Vhaidra was not sure why, but as she had yet another contraction, she wished her husband could be in the same room as her, even though this was neither the human nor the drow way.

About an hour later, the baby was finally born. Vhaidra refused to scream out in pain, no matter how much it hurt. This ability to put mind over matter shocked Valeria completely. Just as Vhaidra had done during the labour, she continued to refuse pain-dulling herbs and healing potions, and just focused on the experience.

The baby was washed, and then, fed from her breast. Finally, the baby was taken to the next room to see her father while the mother was to be washed and dressed.

"Hypodiakonos Nikodemos, what did you want?" asked the midwife.

"A healthy baby!" he replied.

"Well, you got one. Here is your beautiful baby girl!" the midwife said as she presented Nikodemos with his child.

A tear of happiness fell from Nikodemos' eye, and the enchanted moonstone in his left eye socket appeared to glow as he held his daughter for the first time. His daughter stared at her father's moonstone eye and almost appeared to smile.

Congratulations were given to the new father as his wife was cleaned up and dressed in an elegant black velvet dress. Once the new mom was cleaned and ready, Valeria called them in to see Vhaidra.

"Hypo, isn't she beautiful?" Vhaidra asked.

"Yes, of course, she is. While I am not surprised that her skin is dark grey like yours, I am shocked that her hair is black like mine! I thought drow babies only had white hair!"

The midwife interrupted, "I guess anything is possible with half-drows. Look at those pointy ears!"

"Look at her beautiful green eyes!" Vhaidra added.

Green was a colour she hated having her eyes called, but on her daughter, she loved the colour.

"They are almost as beautiful as her mom's chartreuse eyes!" Nikodemos said as he handed the baby girl back to her mother's waiting arms.

The Protopresbyteros started the *first-day prayers* as the parents stared at their lovely beloved daughter.

⸻•◦●◦•⸻

Their daughter was named *Athanasia* on the eighth day, but her mother called her *My Little Crow* because of her dark grey skin and jet-black hair.

⸻•◦●◦•⸻

When Athanasia received the *vaptisma* on her fortieth day, the baby was given a nouna, which was a local elderly human lady, named *Helena*, who unfortunately died two years after Athanasia's birth. Prayers were also offered for Vhaidra at this time as well. They went like this,

"O Ancient of Days, the true Bread of our Life, who have cleansed and regenerated us through Your incarnate dispensation, and have commanded us, Your unworthy servants, to bless and to sanctify those who approach Your holy Name: O Lord our God, purify also Your handmaiden, Vhaidra, through the purification of forty days, and bless her and guard her and the infant, Athanasia, to which she has given birth, and the leaven

of her hands and all the works of her hands, that she may, without hindrance, nurture all in her house according to Your Holy Will, that we may glorify and worship Your infinite goodness in the Creator-Logos-Ghost, now and ever, and unto ages of ages. Amen."

———•◦●◦•———

After Athanasia received the mysteries of The Way, Miriam said her goodbyes to her friends and joined the Transfiguration Cenobium as a novice monk. Her friends came for the initiation rites and congratulated their friend on becoming a monk.

As was traditional of The Way, they took blessings from Archimandrite Olga, the head of the monastery in which Miriam had joined, kissing her hand and asking for her prayers. After they left the monastery, Vhaidra mentioned that she felt like the archimandrite did not want to have her hand kissed by her. Ti'erra felt the same thing, but Nikodemos did not sense anything. Elder Dionysios was not sure who was correct about this and didn't want to judge the archimandrite.

CHAPTER VI

ETYMOLOGY OF THE DROW

YEAR 3

Almost one year later, Vhaidra gave birth again, this time, sadly, to a tiny stillborn baby who was named *Barachial* at his burial. He was dark grey with white hair and pointed ears, like his mother, but had red eyes, unlike either parent.

Vhaidra was very touched by the prayers that were offered when she miscarried her first son. The prayers were very similar to the prayers given to her after she had given birth to her Crow. She often thought of them when she thought of Barachial. They went like this:

"O Ancient of Days, who were born of the Holy Theotokos; so now, according to Your great mercy, have mercy on this, your handmaiden, Vhaidra, whose child has reposed. Forgive all her transgressions, both voluntary and involuntary, and protect her from every oppression of the devils. Cleanse her of every sin and heal her sufferings. Grant her health and strength of soul and body, and encompass her with bright and radiant angels. Preserve her from every approach of invisible spirits. Yea, O Lord, preserve her from sickness and infirmity. Cleanse her bodily afflictions and inward travail. By Your quick mercy, lead her to recovery. And with trembling, we cry out and say, 'Look down from the Heavens and behold our helplessness.' And, according to Your great mercy, as the Good God and the Lover of Mankind, have mercy on her, through the prayers of your most-pure mother, and of all the Saints. For to You are due all glory, honour, and worship: to the Creator-Logos-Ghost, now and ever, and unto ages of ages. Amin."

———◦•●•◦———

YEAR 4

A little over a year after that, the couple had another boy, this time a thin, live-born child named Damianos. He was a medium grey skin tone with very light brown hair that they called dirty blonde. His ears were the same shape as his father's, and he had green eyes just like his sister. His skin was unique for an elf, because as they found out when he got older, the more sun exposure he had, the darker his skin became.

———◦•●•◦———

YEAR 5

Another year later, she had yet another boy, a very thick baby who was named Kosmas. He was her biggest baby yet. He was so big that he barely made it out without dying. But he had a fighting spirit and made his way out in one piece. His birth was the hardest on Vhaidra and caused so much damage to her womb that she would unfortunately never be able to have children again. He looked fully human with very pale, light but barely grey skin, light—almost platinum—blonde hair, but very pointed ears and yellow eyes. Some humans mistook him for a *high elf*. Vhaidra thought that was strange, since he obviously had the bulkier body structure of a large human, just like her husband, Hypo.

He did not have even the slightest hint of the elven slight build. To her, Kosmas looked like a human with elven ears and eye-colour. Both Kosmas and Damianos had Elder Dionysios as their *nounos*, just like Mikhail, making them all *adelfoi*, which meant they were all brothers in spirit, even if they were not blood brothers with Mikhail.

After getting the diagnosis that she would no longer be able to have children, Vhaidra asked if, since she would no longer be getting pregnant each year, the stretch marks would fade.

The midwife replied, "No, Vhaidra. While they may fade, they never fully go away. Remember that your belly skin was stretched more than a drow would normally stretch and in a shorter time than your body would be used to. But I always tell my patients to think of them as battle scars that they can be proud of."

"I like that thinking, Valeria. Those are the perfect words to comfort a drow. We are a vain race when it comes to beauty, but every dark elf is proud of the scars it retains from a successful battle."

"You have retained your beauty well; it has been my honour to be your midwife."

"I will miss having you around, Valeria."

"I will miss being your midwife and helping you give birth to these beautiful children," Valeria replied and gave Vhaidra a hug, which inexplicitly made Vhaidra cry.

Nikodemos had insisted, since Athie's birth, on Vhaidra giving the children an elven *middle name*. This name was a second name that would go between their name given to them from The Way on their eight-day and their family name of Iroas. Her husband said this would help connect them to their mother and their elven ancestry. While it was not completely unusual for humans to have middle names, it was a much stranger practice for a drow.

Vhaidra, however, reacted to this unique request very seriously. She explained that she would need to pick the names very carefully, as drow legend was that the meaning of one's name was intimately tied to their destiny and could alter their lives. Nikodemos was not sure whether this was true but honoured her worries with acceptance of her process. After each child was named by The Way on their eighth day, he would tell her the meaning of the child's name, and Vhaidra would try to find a drow name that meant close to the same thing, so as not to alter their destiny as assigned by The Ancient of Days and his clergy.

Since the name Athanasia meant *eternal life*, Vhaidra gave her daughter a middle name meaning the same thing, *Quarae*. Barachial was posthumously given the middle name of *Altonerd*, as both names meant *lightning of god*. Damianos' and Kosmas' names were not so easily translated to a drow name, so Vhaidra came up with the closest translations that she could. Damianos, which meant *to tame*, was given the middle name of *Elkaugh* which meant *chaos breaker*. Kosmas, which meant *beautiful order* was given the middle name of *Masvayas* which meant *beauty forger*.

Realising that names were so important to drow culture after Vhaidra gave Athanasia her middle name, Nikodemos asked her about the meaning of her name and the names of her family members. She explained that Vhaidra meant *deep lover*, while her mother's name, *Brizinil*, meant *graceful lady*, and her father's name, *Alakzar*, meant *best mate*, while her house name meant *heirs to dominance*.

Nikodemos had never heard about Vhaidra's mother or father before and was shocked to hear her speaking about them at this time. Having lost his parents and only brother in his youth, which led to a period of deep darkness for Nikodemos, he hadn't spoken of his family either. In the past, he would not dare ask her about her parents unless she would have brought up the subject first, as he knew firsthand how the loss of parents could cause a lot of pain and troubles.

Avoiding that subject of Vhaidra's parents, Nikodemos told her that he thought her name was fitting, as her love was so deep and he loved her deeply as well. However, she let him know it more likely meant *loving the deep lands of the underworld*, although she was now open to that novel definition of his as well.

Vhaidra was not surprised at all that Nikodemos' name meant *victory of the people* and that his family name, which she now shared, meant *chosen* or *hero*. This name of her family's house was very auspicious to her eventual return to the underworld to get revenge on the house that had usurped hers.

———— •●•●•●•• ————

This initial conversation also caused Nikodemos and Vhaidra to talk with their friends about this, out of curiosity, and to ask them the meanings of their names, to see if they had matched up to their destiny so far.

They found out that Ti'erra's given name meant *oath tree* in the dwarven language and *magic singer* in the language of the wood elves. The couple was not sure how this matched up to her destiny so far. What really fascinated the Iroas family is that they learned that dwarves do not have a family name; they have a surname that they choose for themselves based off of something they do or named after their weapon or armour. She told them that she would give them three guesses to guess the surname that she had recently taken on for herself.

Nikodemos guessed, "So, is your surname Hammerdancer?"

"No, but good guess!" Ti'erra replied.

Vhaidra guessed second, saying, "Is it Littlebeauty?"

"No, but I like your guess too. One guess remaining. So, I'll give you a hint. Just like Miriam, my given name and surname begin with the same letter."

Vhaidra immediately blurted out, "Toughpretty?"

Ti'erra laughed, liking their guesses. "Monk and Cleric, I like your guesses, but I just recently took the name on something I recently acquired. I am now Ti'erra Turtlearmour."

"Oh, I like that!" Nikodemos explained.

"Well, at least, it tells that you are tough. So, I got that right. But really, your new armour you took and had altered from the Battle for Sicyon is more important to you than your hammer or dancing?"

"Let's just say that once I found it, I felt that its destiny and mine were attuned to each other."

"Well, that is really amazing, Ti'erra Turtlearmour," Vhaidra exclaimed.

The couple also found out that Miriam's given name meant *sea of bitterness and sorrow,* which both Vhaidra and Nikodemos agreed that it had matched her fate to date. They already knew that her surname or family name started with the letter M from their discussions with Ti'erra. However, later, they learned from Miriam herself that it was Mosseri, which meant that her husband's family was originally from the land of Misr. Even though they most recently had lived in the city of Halab, the capital city of Suria.

Elder Dionysios' name meant *belonging to the light of the tree,* which confused both of them, but he had assured them that it was very befitting to him as the guardian of the Armour of the Ancient of Days. Lastly, Mikhail's name meant *gift from god.* They would learn how very fitting this name was in the future. As an orphan and a monastic of The Way, Elder Dionysios did not have a surname or family name (surnames or family names were given up as a sacrifice to The Ancient of Days when a novice monk joined a monastery, showing their separation from the world) and neither did Mikhail.

From these discussions, Nikodemos became convinced that perhaps a child's name could actually affect the destiny of a child after all, in some situations. He actually started reading stories about ancient heroes and looked up the meaning of their names to see if they matched up with their final destinies. Most of them did not, but he supposed this happened more often in drow culture if meanings were so important to them.

He started looking for how the lives of his children matched up with their names. He wondered with Athanasia's name meaning of eternal life if somehow, she would one day inherit the Armour of The Ancient of Days, which was now internalised within his bones – the very armour that had seemingly stopped his ageing.

He also looked to see if Damianos would learn to tame animals, and perhaps, Kosmas would become a jeweller. His suppositions of the meanings of the names of his living children would prove to be completely incorrect in the end.

He figured Barachial's name signified the short amount of time (lightning was only around for a flash) that he was with them, living less than a year within Vhaidra's womb before he was stillborn.

CHAPTER VII

A POX ON BOTH YOUR HOUSES

Vhaidra asked about Nikodemos' parents shortly after she had first given Athanasia her middle name of Quarae, and they had talked to their friends about the meanings of their names. She had never met his parents, but that was not something she thought as unusual, being a dark elf.

"Hypo, you never speak of your parents, and I always thought that humans continued a relationship with their parents after adolescence?"

"Dear, my parents are dead."

"What happened to them?" Vhaidra asked.

"My father, Tomas, was a great hunter but was killed by a bugbear when I was fourteen. He came over the top of a mountain into a nest of baby bugbears just as the mother was returning from gathering food for them."

"Oh, no! I hear they go into a rage when they think their children are threatened."

"Indeed, but they are also experts at ambushing people too, and that is what unfortunately happened to my father."

"An ambush?"

"Well, sort of. He was backing up, reaching for his bow, but also trying to make himself look both large and as unthreatening as possible, repeating over and over, 'Good bugbear, good bugbear!' – as we are taught to do in such a situation. However, as he was doing this, the father bugbear snuck up behind him and bashed his skull in before he even knew what happened."

Listening carefully, Vhaidra raised a question, "Since you know what happened, I am guessing he was not alone and there was a witness?"

"Yes, he was not alone. He was with his brother, my uncle Tobias, who saw what happened and fled for his life. My mother, Charissa, blamed him for not having my father's back or even killing the bugbear assailant.

She did not only do this privately, but publicly in the street, and embarrassingly, even in the Temple of The Way. Because of this, my uncle, in shame and unable to escape her constant attacks on his character, left the country. We never heard from him again."

"Do you blame him, Hypo?"

"No, dear. I don't blame him for leaving. He obviously felt guilty, and then, my mother harassing him had to make it one hundred times worse for him!"

"No, Hypo. I mean, do you blame him for your father's death?"

"Oh! No. I mean I did at first, led by my mother's condemnations. Later, I realised, using logic rather than emotion, that it came down to one question – what could he have done? He could have done what I did later, and tried to kill the father bugbear, but then, he would have had to kill the mother bugbear too, and then the babies would be left on their own to die or have to be killed as well. Killing them would not bring him back, which I only can see now that I am older."

"Wait, did *you* try to kill the bugbears?"

"Yes. Seeing my mother's grief and despair, I went out with my brother, Odysseus, and hunted down the bugbear."

"You have a brother?"

"Had," Nikodemos sadly retorted.

"What happened?"

"Well, we went and found the bugbears, and we started killing them. As I killed the mother bugbear, my brother attacked the father bugbear. Sadly, Odysseus' bow broke, and with no other weapon available other than his hunting dagger, he charged the father bugbear, going into a rage, embedding his hunting dagger in its chest. Unfortunately, the beast was able to kill Odysseus with a ferocious series of bites before it died a slow, painful death from the deep dagger wounds."

"So, you lost your father and your brother to the same bugbear?" Vhaidra asked, shocked.

"Yes. Killing all those bugbears didn't bring our father back at all. Instead, it made me lose my brother and my mother!"

"Wait, your mother was there too?"

"No, but after I had returned from our wholesale massacre of all those bugbears, with her having now lost both her husband and youngest son, she fell into a deep depression. Shortly thereafter, she killed herself."

"I'm so sorry that you lost your family in such a horrible way for you, Hypo."

"It was a very painful part of my life, but thankfully, time helps heal all wounds eventually."

"So, you are no longer angry about those bugbears being the cause of your family's death?"

"I wish it never happened, but what good will anger do for me? Revenge only made things worse and made me lose more. The Way helped me understand that, and I am now at peace with what happened."

"Interesting. Not to change the subject, but what did your family members' names mean?" she asked, trying to see if their names linked to their final destiny.

"Odysseus means *to hate*, Tomas means *twin*, and Charissa means *kind and gracious*."

"Oh, was your father a twin?"

"No, not at all. Although he did look very much like his older brother, Tobias. I don't think its meaning is why he was given this name by The Way."

"What did Tobias' name mean?"

"It means, *God is good*."

Vhaidra did not speak it aloud but secretly wondered if Odysseus' name showed that his hatred of the bugbears was intertwined with his name's meaning and his destined death.

"What did you do after your mother's death?" Vhaidra asked her husband, going back to the prior subject.

"I went through a very dark time. Thankfully, I was old enough to live on my own, and my family had some wealth. So, I did not have to apprentice somewhere in exchange for table scraps and a roof over my head."

"What was this time of darkness?"

"I honestly don't know. I left the city with a group of the *Beta Phi Sigma Alpha Explorers*, and we killed some creatures threatening a nearby town at first, but my bloodlust was not easily satiated. I ended up leaving that group of adventurers and joining another group that called themselves the *Tau Lambs*, who were extremists filled with hatred like I was. But that is the last thing that I remember, until I awoke one day, a year later, in a pool of blood and dead creatures all around me, as well as all of the corpses of the Tau Lamb adventurers that I had been with."

Nikodemos continued, "I came to, bleeding badly. I realised that I was being taken care of by a wandering group of monks of The Way, called *pilgrims*, who were moving from their previous city of residence to a establish a new monastery in the desert, away from worldly cares. They are the ones that helped me mentally, emotionally, and spiritually heal from my trauma – which only was worsened by my bloodlust. The pilgrims told me that sometimes when the mind is injured and troubled, the body is unaware and can't heal the mind until the body is also injured and the entire person needs to be healed and made whole again. Only then can both healings happen concurrently."

"Interesting. Do you wish to regain your missing memories?"

"I am not sure that I do. I think there is probably a good reason that I do not remember. Perhaps The Ancient of Days is protecting me from something horrible that I do not wish to relive."

"Mayhap," Vhaidra replied, "Mayhap, Hypo."

"So, hey, neither one of us have really spoken of our parents before. Does speaking about yours cause you any emotional trauma?"

"No, not at all. We do not necessarily have the same attachment to house members in the underworld as you have here in the overworld. Sure, I have this attachment now to my family up here, but down there, I never did."

"Okay, because now I am really confused. Why do you have a strong desire to have revenge on the house that supplanted your former house?"

"It is a matter of honour, Hypo. House honour is more important to a drow, especially a female drow, than blood."

Learning this, Nikodemos finally grappled the courage to ask his wife about her parents, "So, what happened to your parents then?"

"I'm honestly not sure, Hypo. When I finally got done battling my way out of Xunquarra Skete, I went to the estate of my house and there were not very many survivors left. I heard that my mother was dead. My father was not amongst the survivors that escaped with me, as far as I could tell."

"So, he could potentially still be alive?" her husband queried.

"I suppose it could be. If so, he would probably now be part of another house, serving them."

"Do you long to see him again?"

"Not really, Hypo. As I said before, we didn't really have the concept of love or even the overworldly familial familiarity in the underworld."

"If my father was still alive, I would want to find him."

"But not your uncle Tobias?" Vhaidra replied.

"Fair point. I guess I never thought about it, just like you never thought of looking for your father." Changing the subject, Hypodiakonos Nikodemos then asked, "By the way, how long were your mother and father together? I know there aren't marriages in the underworld amongst the drow."

"Yes, you are right, Hypo. In the underworld, children are not born of love, and there is no such thing as marriage like there is in the overworld. So, my father, *Alakzar*, was simply a male drow that, for a while, at least, found favour with my mother, the Matron Mother of *House Oussviir*. I'm not sure how he was able to find favour for so long, as he and my mother stayed together for at least twenty years after my birth, and they had been together for many years beforehand as well. Not only that; he was allowed to survive after he was thrown out of the matron's chambers."

"Did they have any other children?"

"No. I was the matron mother's only child birthed by her."

"Why was he thrown out?"

"Well, I am not completely sure, to be honest. I do remember that when I was around twenty years old,

I heard my mother yelling at my father. Then, he was taken and beaten publicly, but not killed. He was then taken to the house dungeons for many years. So, I did not see him for a long time. After that, it was only on occasion, but since children are only seen as the property of their mother, he did not really have much of anything to do with me after that time."

"What about before he was exiled to the dungeons of *House Oussviir?*"

"From what I can recall, which admittedly is not much, I remember him actually being kind to me."

"Well, I am glad to hear that at least."

With that, Vhaidra just smiled at her husband, looking in his caring eyes, glad that she had met him and had been introduced to love by him. She put her hand upon his chin and pulled his face to hers so she could kiss him. That kiss was interrupted by the sound of Athanasia's cries of hunger.

———◆———

After Athie was fed, Vhaidra had another question for her husband, "So, you keep asking about my father. What was your father like, Hypo?"

"Honestly, he was the very epitome of a 'manly' man. He had huge muscles and was very strong. When he was young, he, along with his brother, Tobias, played *choule*, a violent team game with a ball, where one city's men would take on another city's men, trying to score the most points. One time, he slammed his head into another player so hard that the other player was knocked out dead!"

"That sounds like a game that drows would like to play!" Vhaidra excitedly added.

"Eventually, the game was banned in Hellas, and my father switched to *kolv*, a game of hitting a sack of dried beans with a club to a hole in the ground that was very far away. The men who hit it in the least amount of swings would claim all the gold that the players would put in a pot in order to play."

"That does not sound like a drow game at all, not violent enough!" she added with a laugh. "However, betting on who wins, that is something my people would definitely do!"

"I never played it. Although I did play the forbidden game of choule with friends out in fields when I was an adolescent."

"Did you ever get hurt like your father?"

"Not too badly, but once I launched another player way up high in the air. Although he got knocked out, we actually became good friends after that."

Vhaidra laughed at that comment, saying, "Everyone wants a powerful friend." and then, asked, "What else were your parents like?"

"Well, my father worked a lot. He was a deliveryman for the far southern branch of the *Hanseatic League*, delivering packages all over the country. He was gone a lot, but always found time to teach us how to hunt as he was an expert marksman. This skill also had enabled him to fend off would-be-thieves during his deliveries."

"What was his weapon of choice?"

"He liked bows and arrows. For deliveries, he would use poisoned arrowheads against would-be thieves, but for hunting, he would use regular ones."

"So, did you become proficient with the bow?"

"Unfortunately, no. So, eventually, after getting tired of my constant archery failures, my father bought me a crossbow, and I used that for hunting until I travelled to Zhong and received my Yan Yue Dao, *Qing Long*, which was really more my style. I liked using that as both a ranged weapon and a melee weapon as well."

"Interesting! Before I joined the monastery, I used to have tiny hand crossbows that I wore on my wrists." Vhaidra replied.

Nikodemos was intrigued, "Those must have been interesting to use!"

"Well, they are kind of a standard weapon for drows."

"Used for assassinations or for hunting, dear?" he laughed.

"Both," Vhaidra replied, "Anyway, I'm glad that your father taught you to hunt, or you may have never been out in that forest to save me from those high elves when I brought my house out from the underworld."

"May The Ancient of Days be praised!" Nikodemos replied.

"And your mother?"

"May she be praised too?" he said unsurely.

"No, I mean tell me about her!" Vhaidra laughed.

"She was always baking, helping us with our studies and such. She was your typical mother, making sure we tried to learn to play music; that we went to the temple each week and did our best in our studies. She beat us if we failed in any of these activities."

"What about your brother, Odysseus?"

"Honestly, we really fought a lot. He was a born berserker. So, we had some crazy fights. It is probably how he was still able to kill that bugbear with only a hunting dagger while it was killing him."

"Berserker? I have heard of duergars being berserkers, but we did not have them amongst the drows that I knew in the dark city of *Olath Che'el* in the underworld. What is it like when humans go into berserker mode?"

"My brother would grow larger, turn ruddy, his lips would curl back, and he would start swinging, either bare-fisted or with a dagger! When he was in a rage, he had no idea what he was doing, and after it was over, he would lay on the ground panting, often falling asleep where he laid. When he woke up, he would have no memory of it. When his friends or I would try to tell him about his actions, he never believed us either!"

"Wow! How did you deal with fighting him when he was in berserker rage?" Nikodemos' wife asked.

"I would try to calm him down at first, but eventually, he would get a lucky hit on me and draw blood. Then, I was done with trying to make peace. Since it was all adrenaline and he wasn't strategically thinking, I would go on the defensive and look for a pattern in the chaos, and when I had an opening, I would grab his arms and pin them behind him with one hand, and in the other hand, I would slam his head into the ground or another object until he lost consciousness."

"Wow, now that sounds like a drow sibling relationship!" Vhaidra added.

"I can only imagine! It really taught me the importance of strategy. That's why I appreciate Ti'erra so much. She always has a strategy in battle."

"So, did you still have the love of *storge* or *philia* for your brother even though you fought all the time?"

"Of course, it may sound weird, but yes, and I was always protective of him as my younger brother. It was one thing if I was fighting him, but if others tried to mock or fight him, I always had his back."

"Very interesting, Hypo. Let's go to bed now."

"Good idea," he replied, following her to their marital bed.

What Nikodemos did not know is that his uncle Tobias had fled to the far northern land of Rus'. When Nikodemos and Odysseus were fighting the bugbear family, their guardian angels had flown to him and asked him to pray for them. As he prayed, The Ancient of Days allowed him to see the entire battle happen and watch his nephew die on the same hand as Tobias' brother had. In tears, he asked for forgiveness of The Ancient of Days and asked what he must do to properly repent and become right in the eyes of his god since he now also felt responsible for his nephew's death. After all, had he killed those bugbears, his nephews would not have felt the need to go out and there and magnify the tragedy.

He asked and he received. He heard the word of the Creator-Logos-Ghost, and doing what he was told, he became a hermit ieromonk of The Way near the city of Nizhny in the faraway land of Rus'. Every day, he prayed to The Ancient of Days all day, stopping only to sleep two hours a day and to eat whatever food was given to him as alms. During his prayers, Tobias asked for the protection of his only surviving nephew, Nikodemos. These prayers without ceasing were what was responsible for his nephew, now a hypodiakonos, surviving the dark times he had experienced after losing all of his family, returning to The Way, finding his clerical calling and making it back on the dangerous trip he had taken to the land of Zhong as well as in the many troubling days since then.

Unbeknownst to any of them, Tobias' prayers had also helped Hypodiakonos Nikodemos and his friends when they fought in the Battle for Sicyon.

CHAPTER VIII

A LONG PAINFUL DEATH BY ORC

YEAR 6

A year after the birth of Kosmas, an elderly woman named Sophia arrived in Sicyon, looking for Elder Dionysios. Although she lived far away, she had heard of his becoming the guardian of The Ancient of Days and his part in the Battle for Sicyon, along with being the spiritual adviser for the Chosen of The Way. It was a story that had been carried throughout the land, and as stories are, they had been changed, exaggerated and even twisted by some tellers.

Sophia had asked around, and people said he was rarely seen around town, but that the residents of *Omorfia Dipla Sto Potami* would probably be able to help her. She planned on going there, but first, stopped at The Pink Wyrm Tavern to get food and drink before hiking to the edge of the city, where people told her Omorfia Dipla Sto Potami was located.

There, she met Ti'erra, who had heard she was asking about Elder Dionysios.

"Miss, I heard you are asking about the Wizard?" she asked Sophia.

"No, I am looking for Elder Dionysios, the hermit. I have learned that the residents of Omorfia Dipla Sto Potami may be able to tell me how to get in contact with him."

"Oh, yes. The Monk and the Cleric definitely can do that, but so can I, as I am his friend."

"The Great Elder is friends with a tavern dancer?" she asked, shocked.

"He is gracious, he is kind, and he does not judge!" the dwelf replied.

"Would you mind taking me to him?"

"Sure, I can do that, but why, may I ask, do you want to meet him?"

"It has been sixty-six years since I laid eyes on him last. I want to make my peace with him before I repose."

"Make peace with him? How would you have enmity with the Wizard if the last time that you laid eyes on him was when he was a baby?"

"I told you that I am looking for the Elder, not the Wizard!"

"They are one and the same!" Ti'erra explained.

"Oh, okay. Well, it is a long story!"

"I have the time."

"Very well then. Dionysios ruined my life."

"How can a baby ruin your life?" the dancer asked.

"Well, after his birth, I was stigmatised. No man would marry me. Not only because of my son but also because I could no longer produce heirs for them. I have long suffered because of him!" Sophia replied.

"Wait? You are his mother?"

"Yes, I am."

"He knows nothing about you, other than you were a diminutive human woman! And now I see, you are not even that much taller than me. How could you have abandoned him as you did?"

"I did no such thing!" Sophia spat, defensively, although feeling guilt at the accusation. "I was only thirteen years old; I had no husband, my family had been killed by the orc that had left me in my condition, and I had no income. How could I raise a pariah of a child that was half-orc, the very enemy race that had killed my family?"

"I guess that would be hard. Not all half-race children can be raised like I was."

"What exactly are you?" Sophia asked.

"I am a dwelf."

"What is a dwelf?"

"It is half-dwarf, half-elf."

"How did that happen?"

"Well, my mother is a gold dwarf, and once upon a time, the gold dwarves were fighting a common enemy with wood elves. After the battle, there was much drinking of dwarven ale, and one thing led to another, and that led to me being born three years later!"

"Oh, your mother and father courted, married and had you years later?"

"No, I have no idea who my father is. He is one of many Sylvan who shared a bed with my mother that night."

"Oh, my! But three years later? I do not understand."

"Dwarves are pregnant for four years before they give birth while elves and pregnant for two years before giving birth. So, dwelves live in the womb for around three years before being born."

"Interesting! I wonder if that is why I gave birth to Dionysios after only seven and a half months."

"Mayhap; I hear Orcs only live in the womb for six months and often have multiple births from what I understand. Did the wizard have a twin?"

"Oh, heavens no! My womb was already destroyed by Dionysios. I probably would have died if he had been a twin!"

"I am sorry to hear that. Anyway, I do not understand how you can hate your own flesh and blood. He is the most amazing man I know. The wizard has changed my life for the better. In fact, if not for him, I would still be a slave, this city would have been completely ravaged by the evil Jet Fist Cult, and my best friend would have never found her husband!"

"I heard that he was instrumental in saving the city, but I didn't know if the legendary stories were true. Asking around about him today, I have learned that he turned out to be quite the hero after all. Hence, the reason that I need to make my peace with him before I shed this mortal coil."

"You are going to die?"

"Of course, my sweetie. I am seventy-nine years old. That is very long for someone with as rough a life as me. Now, can you lead me to him?"

"Sure. My shift ends in one hour, and then, I will take you to Omorfia Dipla Sto Potami, where we can travel to go meet the Wizard."

"Why do we need to go to Omorfia Dipla Sto Potami?"

"It is the only way that we can get to him without getting the permission of the Episkopos, and that can take days!"

"Thank you, Ti'erra. I am glad that I met you."

"I'm sure it was destiny. Please enjoy your meal, and when I am done dancing, we will go visit the monk and the cleric."

Sophia wondered who the monk and the cleric were. She supposed it must be the rectory for the local Temple of The Way. She expected to meet an ieromonk or ierodiakonos and a presbyteros. She was definitely in for a surprise!

CHAPTER IX

THE ELDER MOTHER

After her shift, Ti'erra bathed in a tavern tub, and changed back into a green smock dress with brown trim, having her armour in her bag. She only wore her armour on adventures and for dancing, as the men found her fascinating, when going from fully armoured to mostly exposed while she danced at the Pink Dragon Tavern.

"Thank you again, Ti'erra, for taking me to Omorfia Dipla Sto Potami."

"No problem. Is that the rest of your meal that you have wrapped up in that cloth?"

"Yes, it was simply too much for me. I'll eat the rest later."

"Just give it to a wandering dog. I am sure the monk will cook for you. She's a great cook!"

Now, Sophia was very confused. A female monk living with a cleric of The Way? '*How abhorrent!*' she thought to herself.

"Hmm, okay," Sophia said to the dwelf.

Her son obviously had very interesting friends. She would soon learn how unique they truly were.

When Ti'erra reached the door, she pulled the rope that rang a bell. The hypodiakonos answered the door and greeted Ti'erra and Sophia.

"Hello, Ti'erra. Who is your friend?"

"Hello, Cleric. This is Sophia, the Wizard's mother."

While Nikodemos was used to Ti'erra addressing the Elder as 'Wizard,' he did not understand that she meant that this was Elder Dionysios' mother.

"Hello, I am Hypodiakonos Nikodemos. Please come in. Can we get you something to eat or drink?"

"No, thank you. I just had a meal," Sophia replied.

They walked into the parlour, where a dark elf in a black dress was breastfeeding a male half-elf while two older half-drow babies ran around the room.

"Oh, we have guests?" Vhaidra exclaimed, surprised to see her best friend with an elderly human female.

"Monk! So nice to see you and Kosmas doing so well. This is Sophia, the wizard's mother."

"Ti'erra, by the wizard, do you mean Elder Dionysios?" Vhaidra asked, inquisitively.

"Yes, who else? What other wizards do I pal around with?" the dwelf replied with a giggle.

Nikodemos was shocked and added, "Oh, my! I should go get him."

"Yes, please do," Sophia responded.

The hypodiakonos went to the seraphim-cherubim-ophan wheel and spun it, opening a secret door, and walked through.

"My son lives in the wall of this manor?" Sophia asked aloud, to no one in particular.

"No, he is the spiritual adviser to my husband and me. He lives in a catacomb hermitage, and we have a magical path that leads from our home to his."

Sophia was way too confused now. How was it that a female monk was married to a cleric and they had children? Wasn't the point of monasticism to be dedicated to the point of almost being married to one's god?

She could hold her tongue no longer and blurted out, "How is it that a monk can be married and have children? I do not understand this at all!"

Vhaidra laughed and explained the situation, "I am a martial monk from the underworld. We dedicate ourselves to the martial arts of war, and yes, we do not marry. I am no longer a member of any monastery, but I am a martial warrior that is best described as a monk."

"So, you are not a monk of The Way?"

No, I am a simple follower when it comes to our faith. My husband is a hypodiakonos. Elder Dionysios is our spiritual guide."

"That explains things much better. I was very confused," Sophia continued with obvious irritation in her voice, looking at Ti'erra, "The way you identify people is very confusing!"

"Sorry, you were confused. Chalk my idiolect up to the parlance of the gold dwarves."

"Well, I certainly have learned a lot today."

"As have we all, apparently," boomed Elder Dionysios' voice from behind them all, asking, "Are you Sophia?"

CHAPTER X

THE WHITE DRAGON'S BITE

Elsewhere, in the far northland called *Jorvik*, the last clan of the *Varangians*, led by *Jerrik*, the king they called *Frea*, made their final plans of attack for their twelve-year insurrection.

His wife, their queen, *Magnhild* asked, "Why do we have to plan twenty-five years' worth of manoeuvres? This seems so unnecessary!"

"We listen to the prophets; we follow the plan of attack. We send our dragons and decimate the towns that we will raid for thirteen years or until they abandon the town. We will only then make land there and attack the bigger cities, catching them unawares!"

"But we only have one dragon left, and it is just a white wyrmling!"

"A wyrmling that will grow and be a full-sized dragon in not too many years, thanks to Gothi Asger!

Wife, we must have patience, just like I have patience with you not giving me a child yet. The prophecies say that after many years of bareness, you shall bear a child, and he shall be called *Sigurd*. Butter and honey, shall he eat, so that he may not refuse the wrong and choose the good. For the child shall know to refuse the wrong and choose wisely. Then, the land whose two kings thou abhor shall be forsaken. You have not fulfilled your requirements, yet I still am patient with you and the prophecies!"

"Aye, we can learn much from your patience, oh, Frea!" said a female *pixie* fluttering near the king.

"Aye!" sounded all the council of the Varangians.

Queen Magnhild was embarrassed and stormed out of the council room. *'Jerrik, you will not have any child conceived tonight or anytime in the near future after embarrassing me like that!'* she muttered to herself, kicking a stone into the nearby sea.

"Thank you, my clansmen. My son, Sigurd, will be born and after fifteen years, he will take my place as your *Drotten*. He will lead us to the most perfect victory that the world has ever seen. But to make this happen, we must follow the path of our fathers and prophets. We must plan well in advance!"

"Aye!" The council yelled again, raising their cups.

"So, after the other attacks previously discussed, we will next send *Ormr* to here in twelve years!" Frea Jerrik yelled out, stabbing a dagger into the map of the seaside city of Sicyon, "From here, we can lay waste to Corinth and then, on to *Athinas*!"

"Aye!" The council yelled once more, raising their cups.

"*Gothi Asger,* go ready Ormr and the ship, and take him to on our twelve-year path of destruction"

"Aye, my Frea!"

Asger the council's shaman left the council meeting and did as he was asked, preparing the ship that would hide the young white dragon until they reached their targets.

"May the gods ever be with you, old Asger!" Jerrik prayed aloud.

The pixie, a one-foot tall female with four wings fluttered up to the frea's ear and whispered something to him.

Frea Jerrik replied, "Very good, Tana. Very good indeed! You are a wise adviser to the Varangians of today, and will be a wise adviser to my son, Drotten Sigurd, in the future as well!"

"I will do my best, Frea Jerrik!" she exclaimed in a high-pitched voice, and then, raced out to look for Magnhild, to try to calm her down.

This would be no easy task. The hot-blooded queen of the Varangians was a very emotional and long-remembering woman.

CHAPTER XI
THE HATED HALF

"Yes, I am Sophia," Dionysios' mother replied and turned around to see the half-orc elder standing with Hypodiakonos Nikodemos.

"I understand you desire an audience with me?"

"Yes, may we speak somewhere private?" she asked, as Damianos ran by her, squealing in delight and chasing his big sister, Athanasia.

"Sophia, the rest of us will just retire to the *solar*. Please stay seated. Hypo, can you get them some tea?"

"Yes, dear."

"Ti'erra, can you grab Damianos?"

"Sure thing, Monk."

"Crow, let's go to the solar!"

"Yay!" screamed Athanasia.

"Thank you, Vhaidra. I appreciate you giving an old woman some private time with her son."

"Your son?" Elder Dionysios asked.

"Yes, Dionysios, I am your mother, Sophia."

"My mother? Why have you come to see me after all these years?"

"Because I have hated you my whole life; that is why!"

"I am very sorry to hear that. Whatsoever have I done to make you feel such a horrible emotion?" the half-orc asked.

"You were born of your father who raped me. You caused me to be barren and unable to have any more children. Your birth made no human man want to touch me, court me, let alone marry me. You caused me so much physical and emotional pain that I left The Way and cursed The Ancient of Days, because he would allow this evil to happen to me. I cried and asked him over and over, why not only did I have to be raped by that monster, the same monster that killed my parents but also to have his bastard son. Why? Why me?"

"I am sorry that life caused you such pain. What would you have me do about this?"

"Once upon a time, I might have asked you to kill yourself so that I could put this horrible thing in my past. In fact, when the stories of you being one of the Heroes of Sicyon reached me, it actually rekindled the fires of my pain. You will never know the pain that I have felt, Dionysios!"

"What would you ask me to do now?"

"Now, I have come to this city to find you. I found a city full of people that admire you. I have found your friends that adore you, especially that slutty dwelf girl. I even heard rumours that you are a mentor to a half-dragon baby at the monastery, one you saved from its evil mother."

"That is true. I believe he is called to be a monk like me."

"Well, until recently, I have only thought of my own suffering, never actually giving a thought about your pain. What pain did you go through, growing in an all-too-small womb? Being given up to an orphanage without ever knowing the love of a mother or father! The pain of having no family; of being different than everyone else. It must have been a very painful childhood, and now, I must admit that you were not to blame for it...I was!"

"Such was my destiny."

"No, it was not destiny. It was my choice. It was a bad, selfish choice of a scared and parentless thirteen-year-old. So, after all these years, and before I die, I want to admit my sin of hating my only son, of not loving you, of throwing you away like trash, and not realising how much pain I caused you."

"Sophia, please do not blame yourself. The Orphanage of the Transfiguration Cenobium was really a good place for me. Yes, other children teased me, but I escaped from that by learning the love of the Creator-Logos-Ghost, and it helped me grow into the man that I am today."

"Nonetheless, I ask your forgiveness and hope that our god will forgive me too."

"Have you spoken to a presbyteros about this?"

"Yes, I did just before I started the journey from Rus' to find you. He said that as part of my repentance, I should find you, share all of my feelings, and ask your forgiveness. Then, and only after I did all that was required for my true repentance could I receive the *koinonia* again."

"Then, you are forgiven, Sophia."

"Can I ask you a favour, Dionysios?"

"What is that you ask?"

"Can you forgive me and call me mother?"

The Elder looked at his mother strangely for a second, tilting his head to the right and back again, and said, "Of course, I forgive you...mother."

"Thank you so much, Dionysios!" she cried, and ran and hugged him.

He slowly and gently put his arms around her, returning the hug.

"Tea is ready!" the hypodiakonos yelled out, coming in the room with a samovar and two teacups.

"Very good! Thank you, Nikodemos!" Sophia said with a smile as a tear ran down her face.

———•◆•———

After many hours of discussion and Sophia and Dionysios getting to know one another, Vhaidra came down, announcing that the babies were all sleeping and that she would be soon making supper.

"Sophia, would you like to stay for supper tonight?"

"No, thank you, Vhaidra. I am going to have Dionysios show me around the Orphanage of the Transfiguration Cenobium where he grew up."

"You just arrived in town. Surely that can wait until tomorrow morning?" asked the dark elf.

Sophia looked up at her son and saw his shrug.

So, she replied, "Sure, I guess that can wait. I won't stay long, as I need to go find an inn. I currently have all my luggage being stored at The Pink Wyrm Tavern."

"No can do; you will stay with me!" shouted out Ti'erra as she bounced down the stairs and then added, "I have an extra room in my home ever since the Ranger joined the monastery. So, you will stay with me."

"I do not wish to intrude!" Sophia objected.

"It would be my honour to house the mother of the Wizard, and I won't take no for an answer."

"Well, I guess I have no choice then, do I?" Sophia laughed.

"Nope, you don't!" the dwelf giggled, and then, explained that she would have Sophia's luggage delivered from the tavern to her home.

Sophia enjoyed the meal and got to know her son's friends better. She said evening prayers with them, as her son lead the group. She wished that it could have gone on forever, but eventually, the babies woke up, and it was time for her to go to Ti'erra's home to sleep.

"Thank you all for an enjoyable evening. I am so glad that my Dionysios has such good friends like you all! I would really be interested in hearing how you all met!"

That night she did learn, as she stayed up with Ti'erra, who told her the whole story of how she had met Vhaidra after the drow had saved Nikodemos, about how Nikodemos saved Vhaidra previously, and how Dionysios got involved as the Guardian of the Armour of the Ancient of Days that the hypodiakonos wore.

The story was exciting and amazing, but it made Sophia sad to figure out that Ti'erra truly loved her son but could never have him since he was sworn to celibacy as an elder monk of The Way. She knew from the story that Dionysios would never break a vow, whether it be to a friend or to their God, The Ancient of Days.

CHAPTER XII

PROPHECY OF THE WOULD-BE-KING

Tana Shimmerwhisper flew after Queen Magnhild as quickly as her little wings would take her.

"Magnhild Freasdotter, you know not to let your temper control you like that!"

"I have a right to my temper. I have the right to be treated kindly. I have a right to be me!" she screamed to the one-foot tall pixie.

"No one denies that you do, but you also must show deference to our wise Frea as his queen!" she replied sternly.

"I am the daughter of our old Frea, and he became king only because he married me. Why should I have to bite my tongue when she earned his title through me?"

"No matter how he earned his kingship, he is truly a wise king that we are blessed to have leading us. Do you not agree, my queen?" Tana said, bowing.

"Yes, Tana," she huffed, "But did he have to publicly embarrass me in front of the entire council, using the prophecy as a weapon?"

"You and I both know that this was not his intent. He simply wanted to remind you that patience was necessary, just like in the fulfilment of the prophecy of the last Varangian King!"

"But do we even know if it is to be our son? It could be a son of another King Jerrik, could it not?"

"The prophecy is very clear that it will be the son of King Jerrik and Queen Magnhild. How likely is this combination to ever come again?"

"I guess you are right," Magnhild sighed, "But how long do we have to wait?"

"Until the One-Eyed decides to make you barren no longer and grant you your son, Sigurd Jerrikson, the Varangian King who will unite us with our enemies, ruling their land and ours!"

"I hope he makes it soon."

"Are you so ready to lose your king and husband?" Tana said with sadness in her voice.

"Let it not be so! I know that according to the prophecy, Jerrik will die shortly after Sigurd takes his journey to manhood with the Princess of the Centauroi. My Sigurd will be more than he seems and will lead the Varangians to Hellas, where he will be declared a hero by those people."

"Strange, isn't it, that a conquering king is welcomed as a hero?"

"Yes, I always found that odd. That, and the part about the Dokkalfar."

Tana shivered, "Ooh, the Dokkalfar! Heinous beasts they are. I am glad that they were long ago finally banished from our lands!"

"Tana, I wish my Sigurd would not have to encounter such a cunning creature. I hope he will be prepared."

"Of course, he will. He has you and Jerrik to guide him in his youth, and the Princess of Centauroi and I to guide him once he is named Drotten Sigurd."

"That does give me hope, my dear friend. Whatever would the Varangians do without you, Tana Shimmerwhisper?"

"I suppose you would all be extinct by now," she joked, winking one of her large eyes.

"Come, let us go prepare the midday meal for our Frea and his Council!"

"Aye, my queen!" the pixie replied with a curtsey.

———— ••◉••• ————

Gothi Asger, the Shaman, had the boat prepared. So, he went home and had a meal with his wife and his son, Kustafr, before he went on the long voyage to many faraway lands that would culminate in Sicyon.

"I wish you both could come with me, but battles on the open sea is not the place for such a fair maiden and child."

"But Asger..."

"But nothing, Gunhild. You know that we must do as the Frea orders so that the Varangians will not go extinct. Make sure that Kustafr learns from the other Gothar so that when I return, he is ready to be my apprentice as the Gothi of the Council."

"Yes, Asger," his wife, Gunhild replied.

"Son, will you be ready to be one of the Gothar when I return?"

"Yes, Father!"

"Good. Practice every day with your Gothar teachers, and be better than anyone else so that no one can deny your rightful place as the council Gothi when I die."

"Yes, Father!"

"That is a good, Son. I will miss you both, but I will carry on knowing that both of you are doing your duties here."

Gunhild asked, "How will we get by without you here?"

"The Council will bring you my wages. I do not need them while on the ship. So, you will get everything. If you need anything, you only need to ask, and they shall provide it."

"Thank you, Asger. May the One-Eyed be with you."

"He will be, but so will the Gods of the Seas, and our living weapon, Ormr the White Dragon as well."

"It was a good thing that my father took those dragon eggs and brought them to the Frea."

"It is unfortunate that in the end that it got him killed, but now, it will ensure that our son and all of the Varangians survive and thrive in this new era."

"May it be so, Asger."

"It shall be, Gunhild, it shall."

With that, Asger he gave his wife and son a kiss and took the bag that she had prepared for him.

"Goodbye, Gunhild. Make sure that when I return, Kustafr Asgerson will be a powerful man and ready to stand at my side."

"I will, Asger."

<hr />

Meanwhile, Queen Magnhild and Tana Shimmerwhisper returned to the council meeting room with their servants to serve the day meal made up of roasted meats, buttered root vegetables, nuts, fruits, rye bread, and plenty of strong mead.

Frea Jerrik called his wife over to stand next to him as he offered a prayer to his Gods and Goddesses,

"Greetings to the virtuous Gods and Goddesses,

Their grateful sons and gracious daughters,

And all from the base to the branches of Yggdrasil,

Who come before us to combine kin and kindness,

Into a caring community of blessed beings.

Let us share this feast and day in honour to you so,

You may share your cup of everlasting wisdom,

Light the various paths we are about to take,

Guide us in the choices we are about to make,

And entwine our destiny for our sake."

He then called for a toast, crying out, "To Queen Magnhild, the most beautiful woman of any land, the mother-to-be of our greatest king, and the finest jewel that the Gods and Goddesses ever forged!"

"To Magnhild Freasdotter!" cried out Tana, and all the men of the council repeated her cry.

The queen smiled at her husband, the king of the Varangians and said, "Thank you, my king."

Frea Jerrik just smiled, patted her thigh, and whispered, "Thank you for being my beloved wife!"

The pixie flew up to Magnhild's ear and whispered, "See, I told you there was no reason to be mad!"

In reply, the queen whispered, "Yes Tana Shimmerwhisper, you are wise beyond your hundreds of years!"

CHAPTER XIII

GET THEE TO A NUNNERY!

Elder Dionysios came to Ti'erra's house in the morning and met Sophia and her for breakfast. Sophia asked if Ti'erra could come with them while he showed her around the monastery and orphanage. Dionysios was glad to have his friend join them and learn more about the Orphanage of the Transfiguration Cenobium as well.

The combination of monastery and orphanage building was a relatively short walk from Ti'erra's house. Miriam answered the door when they knocked, and she was glad to see her friends again. She was very happy to meet the Elder's mother. She took them to Archimandrite Olga to get permission to go for a tour.

Archimandrite Olga was pleased to learn that Elder Dionysios' mother was still alive and had great pity on her. She asked Miriam to take the group on a guided tour of the orphanage and monastery proper and asked Sophia to join her privately after the tour was complete.

Miriam did as she was asked and showed them around. At one point, Mikhail, the half-dragon, came running and hopped up, saying, "Mother Miriam, Mother Miriam!"

Miriam picked him up and introduced the half-dragon to Sophia.

When Mikhail saw the Elder, he proudly recited a prayer that he had learned. Dionysios told Mikhail how smart he was and how proud of him he was.

"I get robes like you now, Elder?"

"Not yet, Mikhail, but keep memorising your prayers every day!"

"I do, Elder, I do!"

"Good boy! Now, go run along and play with the other children, okay!"

"Ok, I do it now! Bye-bye!"

Mikhail hopped down and went running to a group of other children around his age.

"Oh, Dionysios, seeing how that boy wants to please you and the way he is so excited to see Miriam touched my heart so badly. Again, I am so sorry I abandoned you."

"Sophia, please! There is no more need for apologies. I forgive, The Ancient of Days forgives; forgive me a sinner."

Sophia gasped, "You have nothing to ask forgiveness of me for."

"But didn't I ruin your life?"

"That was what I thought, but I see now that I was just being selfish. It's something I intend to make reparations for as best as I can."

"How are you going to make reparations?" Ti'erra asked.

"I plan to live out my life in this monastery, taking care of abandoned children who were given up for their parents. I cannot give my child the childhood he deserved, but mayhap, the Creator-Logos-Ghost will allow me to provide for others that find themselves in the predicament that I put my only son in."

"I think The Ancient of Days would like that," Elder Dionysios smiled.

After taking Sophia back to Archimandrite Olga, Miriam then talked to her friends in the reception hall.

•••••

"Sophia, Ieromonk Tobias sent me a letter, saying that you wish to live out your life in this monastery, taking care of these abandoned children?"

"Yes, I asked for his blessing to do this as part of my repentance."

"Repentance for what?"

"For abandoning my own son when he was a baby."

"Sophia, I have heard of your story, and I think you did not sin by doing what you had to do. I will gladly accept you here, but know that I consider this that you are doing the work that The Ancient of Days willed you to do, and not as repentance."

"Thank you, Archimandrite Olga!"

"In fact, I want to you think that, perhaps, this is what the Creator-Logos-Ghost had planned for your life all along. Mayhap, you have entered into your calling late, but, at least, you finally answered his call."

"I have never thought of it that way."

"Please have Miriam come in, and I will have her set you up in a coenobitic cell. Please give Elder Dionysios and that dwelf my salutations."

"What of my things?"

"You will not need much here, but I will have Miriam go get them. She knows the way, as she once lived with the dwelf. Honestly, I think that is what pushed her into the cenobitic life. Miriam is so orderly and focused on right and wrong, while that dwelf is so wild!"

"Wow! How did you know where I stayed last night?"

"As to how I knew where you stayed, it is my job to know my potential novices," Archimandrite Olga said with a crooked smile.

Sophia left the office and said her goodbyes to her son and Ti'erra, hugging them both. Miriam told them to wait for her as she took the Elder's mother to her cell first, and let one of the senior monks know about the new novice.

Miriam returned and said, "Well, let's go get your mother's stuff then, Elder! And along the way, you can catch me up with all that has occurred outside these walls the last few years!"

They did exactly that, and the Elder and the dwelf walked Miriam back to the monastery after they had collected all of Sophia's worldly belongings.

"It was so nice spending time with you again, Ti'erra," Miriam exclaimed, "Not enough to make me second-guess my monastic calling, but it was nice. I still pray that you convert to The Way one day."

"Mayhap, one day, Ranger, mayhap."

"Elder, please keep praying for me."

"I do, every day, Miriam, every day."

"Thank you, Elder. I appreciate it more than words can say!"

"It is my honour and privilege!" he replied.

CHAPTER XIV

THROUGH THE AERIAL TOLL-HOUSES TO PARADISE OR SHEOL

After three days, Sophia received her robes of a novice monk, and finally, received her koinonia. Then, three days later she died with a smile on her face, the terms of her repentance having been completed and her sins forgiven.

While everyone was very sad for Elder Dionysios, he was actually happy, which confused Ti'erra.

"Ti'erra, Sophia repented of her sins and did everything required of her. As such, her soul will have no troubles passing through the aerial toll-houses on the way to the Shades, where she will experience paradise while she awaits the final judgement."

"Wizard, what are the aerial toll-houses?" she asked.

"When a person dies, their soul separates from the body and gets to see the paradise and the Sheol parts of the shades."

"What is the difference between the paradise and Sheol parts of the shades? And what does that have to do with toll-houses?"

"Paradise was created to be the home of The Ancient of Days' creation but is now a pre-taste of the ten heavens for the souls of those who have reposed. Sheol is a pre-taste of the nine hells. They are the temporal destination of the soul until the final judgement on the last days."

"Oh, paradise is where you want to go then."

"Yes, but you get to experience both. But after the particular judgement..."

"What is the particular judgement?" the dwelf interrupted.

"It is the first judgement of the soul, the judgement where one gets a pre-taste of what may befall it at the final judgement when the body and soul are reunited."

"So, the particular judgement may not be the same as the final judgement?" Ti'erra asked.

"We do not know. That is the decision of The Ancient of Days, and not of us. Just in case, we still pray for those on the journey to their final destination. It is the merciful thing to do. We know that The Ancient of Days exists outside of time. So, we must make the most of our limited time here in prayer."

"So, tell me about these toll-houses, Wizard."

"The demons act as prosecuting attorneys while one's guardian angel acts as the defence attorney. The demons accuse the soul at each toll-house of sins. In some cases, the demon might accuse the soul of sins that they tempted her with, but it didn't comply with, or of sins that she repented for, and in those cases, one of the angels, the one which was the person's guardian angel, speaks for the person, saying that those are lies and that payment is not necessary, taking the soul to the next toll-house. If a person has unrepented sins and does not have enough good deeds and prayers of the living to pay for them, the demons of the corresponding toll-house grab him and take them to Shades to await the final judgement. The twenty toll-houses cover the many sins a soul could be guilty of, including lies, slander, gluttony, laziness, theft, covetousness, usury, injustice, envy, pride, anger, unforgiveness, murder, divination, lust, adultery, unnatural sins, heresy, and unmercifulness."

"What fearful things to be judged for!" the dwelf exclaimed.

"Indeed, Ti'erra, and this is why I always preach of being ready for one's death. We must have a clean conscience by having repented from our sins so that we may temporarily reside in paradise after forty days of death, and eventually, reside on one of the ten heavens with The Ancient of Days after the final judgement."

"Thank you, Wizard. That helps me understand some particularities of The Way more."

"You are welcome, Ti'erra. Will you please stay with me while I read the prayers for the departed?"

"Of course, I will, Wizard!" she replied, grabbed his arm and gave it a little squeeze as she listened to his chant.

"Remember, O Ancient of Days, Your servant, our sister, Sophia, deceased in the faith and hope of life everlasting; and inasmuch as You are good and love mankind, loose, remit and forgive her every voluntary and involuntary transgression, releasing the sins, and destroying the unrighteousness. Deliver her from eternal

torment and the fires of Sheol. Grant her to enjoy and partake of Your eternal bliss prepared for those who love You: for she has sinned, yet she has not rejected You, and has believed without misgiving in the name of the Creator-Logos-Ghost, and has confessed in truth, even to her last breath, oneness with you in unity. Be, therefore, merciful unto her, looking rather upon her works, and since You are bountiful, give her rest with all Your Saints: for there is no one who lives and does not sin, but You alone are without sin, and Your righteousness endures forever; and You are the only God of mercy, and bounty and love for mankind, and to You, we send up glory, to the Creator-Logos-Ghost, now and ever, and unto ages of ages. Amin."

"Why did you call her sister, Wizard?" Ti'erra asked.

"Well, Ti'erra, she may be my worldly mother, but in The Way, we are all brothers and sisters as children of The Ancient of Days."

"Oh, okay! I am not sure that I will ever understand all the complexities of your faith, but I do appreciate you sharing them with me."

"It is my pleasure, Ti'erra."

"Even if I have no intent to convert?"

"Even if..." he replied with a smile, "You know that I do not judge, as that is not my job. I leave judgement to The Ancient of Days alone."

"That is one of the things that I absolutely adore about you, Wizard."

He then patted Ti'erra on the shoulder and asked Ti'erra to allow him some time alone with his deceased mother, Sophia. She was happy to oblige him and go visit the Monk and Cleric.

After Ti'erra left, Elder Dionysios began to chant the psalmody of The Way from the Holy Psalterion.

After three days, the funeral took place and prayers continued for the forty days after death, hoping to help Sophia as she passed through the aerial toll-houses. After these days had passed, Sophia's soul prayed for her son, Dionysios, and his friends while she had her joyful rest in paradise. Dionysios felt the prayers and was very happy that his mother had finally found her happy ending.

CHAPTER XV
FROM NEST TO ROOST

The Iroas children grew up and were occasionally teased at school by some full-blooded human children for being different. Each child handled this differently. Athanasia, or *Athie* as she went by, was a warrior for justice like her father and never let anyone talk down to her or anyone else. Damianos was shy and reserved. Because of this, especially once his ears started to form faint points on them, as he reached puberty. Much to his mother's dismay, he rejected his elven heritage, no matter how much Nikodemos tried to make him appreciate his drow ancestry.

Kosmas was charismatic, and first, tried befriending his bullies, but he was always ready to fight anyone who would try to fight or pick on him, as he was very powerful and could defeat those even twice as big as him. Even though he looked the least drow of all the Iroas children, he loved the dark elven foods the most, never tiring of underworld mushroom dishes.

------- ◦•●•◦ -------

Athie, from a young age and true to her mother's nickname for her, trained to call crows to send messages to her friends around town and to strangers beyond her city to learn about the world around her. She loved to sing and dance with her mother's best friend, Ti'erra. She was blessed to be born with a perfect vocal tone for singing.

------- ◦•●•◦ -------

The Iroas children befriended Mikhail, the orphaned half-dragon, who their parents helped rescue before their births. Mikhail, being different, found solace in The Way, where he was accepted by almost everyone other than a few xenophobic humans. From a young age, he memorised all of the holy books and the hymns of The Way. Many thought he would go on to be a presbyteros, but Elder Dionysios had told him that he thought that instead of that path, that The Ancient of Days wished for him to be a non-cleric monk like himself.

------- ◦•●•◦ -------

Since the children were half-drow, Vhaidra and Nikodemos were not sure if they would age and mature at dark elf speed or human speed, like drow and all other elves aged ten times slower than humans. The local apothecary assured them that all half-elves, and truthfully, almost all half-humans of any type, be it orc, dragon, dwarf, ogre, etc., tended to mature at the human rate.

They were happy, especially Nikodemos, that the apothecary was correct, and all three of their children did not mature at the dark elf rate, but rather at the much faster human rate. Raising children for one hundred forty years would be exhaustive for a human, even one that currently did not seem to be ageing. Vhaidra had told him that while technically it took one hundred forty years for an elf to mature, they were expected to act like an adult far earlier in the underworld. Truthfully, they had expected it to be somewhere in between the two rates, much like their physical features were a combination of both drows and humans.

The children were taught in their home to cook, sew, read, write, exercise, paint, and other skills that they would need later in life. They also attended the schools in Sicyon, both of which were run by The Way. One was for only the boys, and one for only the girls. Female monastics ran the girls' school and male monastics ran the boys' school, even though all the orphans lived at the female monastery's Orphanage of the Transfiguration Cenobium.

At school, the children learned the songs, dogma, and scriptures of The Way. Children that were not of The Way were also allowed to attend if their parents were open to it, but they required the students to attend the divine services of The Way at the Temple. This way, the parents would learn more about the faith, and the clergy hoped that they would join.

———••●••———

This happened with a high elf family that came to Sicyon as their base for adventuring. They adventured with another high elf couple, two wood elf couples, and two gold dwarf couples. Each couple decided to be based out of a different city, where they would get to know the locals, strike up deals with the blacksmith, and get to know the locations near the city. This couple, Larzyr'ss and Zilvara had their daughter attend the local school and had her board at the Orphanage of the Transfiguration Cenobium for a fee when they were out on adventures. Larzyr'ss came to appreciate The Way, as did his daughter, Alexandra, but his wife never appreciated the faith, only worshipping The Protector, the god of high elves.

The high elves had let their daughter choose her name when she was old enough, but she instead let The Way name her at her vaptisma, hence the human name of Alexandra. She so desired to be a human that dyed her hair red with henna, put fake freckles on her face and claimed to be only half-elf. She couldn't always cover her ears completely, but she did try to wear her long hair over them to hide them as much as possible.

The desire of her daughter to be like humans distanced her mother from her even more. This distancing made Alexandra want to be as different as possible from her mother and she came up with a plan to become something that her mother would really hate, a paladin of The Way! Unfortunately for her, The Way only allowed males to become paladins. However, she remained determined to make this happen.

Even though she was one of the few elves in the school, she did not ever befriend the Iroas children, preferring to be only around humans of The Way and eschewing elvenkind.

———✦✦✦———

This also happened with a duergar family who came to Sicyon to make weapons for the overworlders and inquired about having their children attend school to better acclimate them to the overworld culture. The children joined the school, and the parents converted, but rarely attended services after conversion, as blacksmithing was a full-time job every day. They were able to send their kids to the required services along with other families from the school, who they had befriended after the parents purchased the fabulous weapons that the father, TaeLyon, made.

Since the school required non-orphan students to have a surname or family name, the twins used their father's surname of Axenforge. He chose this surname for himself when he was younger and first figured out how to make axes that were not only perfectly balanced for both ranged and melee attacks. When the two twin-siblings were older, as was the dwarven way, they would choose their own surname.

———•••●••———

The school was formatted the same way for both the boys and the girls of The Way in Sicyon. The grade level of schooling was based on the child's date on the first day of the ecclesiastical new year, which was called the *Indiction*, and always fell on the first day of September. There were no exceptions at all, even if the child had a birthday on the day after the new year's first day. This date was chosen, as it was believed that the world had been created by The Ancient of Days on this date. So, they celebrated this date as the new year.

While children would start their new school year on this date, the parents would plant carrots, turnips, onions, leeks, garlic, lettuce, and celery. Two special hymns were chanted at the divine services on this day as well.

"Creator-Logos-Ghost,

Setting times and seasons by Your sole authority,

Bless the cycle of the year of Your grace,

O Ancient of Days,

Guarding our rulers and Your nation in peace,

At the intercession of the Theotokos,

And save us.

You who created all things in Your infinite wisdom,

And set the times by Your own authority,

Grant Your people victories.

Blessing our comings and goings throughout this year,

Guide our works according to Your divine will."

The school grade level to age was as follows:

First grade level for six-year-old children

Second grade level for seven-year-old children

Third grade level for eight-year-old children

Fourth grade level for nine-year-old children

Fifth grade level for ten-year-old children

Sixth grade level for eleven-year-old children

Seventh grade level for twelve-year-old children

Eighth grade level for thirteen-year-old children

The schooling ended after a child's thirteenth year, as this is when they would either be very busy being an apprentice of a trade or could choose to join a monastery as a novice monk. Not all children actually went for all eight years, as their families needed them to start working to help support their household.

YEAR 12

During many of the weekends, Nikodemos and Vhaidra, often accompanied by Ti'erra, and always accompanied by Elder Dionysios, would take their children out to hunt in the woods. They often would take Mikhail, the half-dragon from the local Orphanage of the Transfiguration Cenobium out with them too.

As they got older, they would also sleep in the woods. Here, the children learned how to fell a tree, and then, chop it into firewood and/or wood for shelter. They also learned how to catch fish with spears or their bare hands. As they got older, they also learned survival skills like map reading, what to do if they were lost, or how to heal themselves if they got hurt. Because of this, even though they lived in a very nice stone house fit for royalty, the children knew how to take care of themselves out in the wild.

———✴•●•✴———

It was on one of these trips that Mikhail learned that he could change into a full obsidian dragon, but one similar in size of his normal form.

While they were camping, three orcs wandered into their camp and started using their axes, tearing at their tents that the Iroas family was sleeping in. Athie attempted to attack one of the orcs with two swords, and all she got for her troubles was to be picked up and slammed to the ground, knocking her out. This enraged Vhaidra, who ran to her daughter's defence and used her martial skills to jump up and apply blows to the temple and a few arteries of the beast, incapacitating it and poisoning it. Vhaidra was the rare creature who could actually fight better when she was enraged. The only problem was that not unlike a berserker, she often went too far or did not know when to stop.

———— ···•●•··· ————

Meanwhile, Elder Dionysios grabbed Mikhail and told him to take flight. Confused, he asked the elder what he meant.

"You are a half-dragon. That means you can morph into dragon form. Do it now!"

"But how, Elder?"

"First, focus on the fire in your belly. Next, imagine an obsidian dragon. Then, picture your body changing from how it looks now into that image."

Mikhail did as he was told. He thought it would be difficult, but it was just as easy as bringing a thought to his mind...except it was very painful! Wings sprouted from his shoulder blades and expanded out one metre on either side. Then, his shape changed from humanoid to draconic in shape, and the places where he previously had no scales, soft, dark grey scales filled in.

———— ···•●•··· ————

At the same time, Ti'erra danced around one orc, whistling as she did and when it was confused by the behaviour, she hit one of its knees with her hammer, making it bend the wrong direction and freezing like that. Even though the ice dissipated some of the pain, the beast still howled in pain as he fell to the ground. He would not be in pain long, however, as Hypodiakonos Nikodemos used his Yan Yue Dao to decapitate him shortly thereafter.

⸻ ❋ ⸻

Once Mikhail had fully transformed, he looked at the remaining orc in the eyes and screamed, but instead of sound, the fire that he had imagined in his belly when transforming into an obsidian dragon came billowing out of his mouth and cooked the orc very well done where he stood. The children were shocked to see such a thing, having not known much about the abilities of half-dragons. Nikodemos, Vhaidra, Ti'erra, and Dionysios had once seen him do this before when they were on a ship and Mikhail was just a baby who had been aged to twenty years old by powerful pirate sorcerers.

⸻ ❋ ⸻

Vhaidra called Elder Dionysios to her daughter, Athanasia, and asked him to start healing her. Luckily, she did not have any long-lasting issues from the powerful slam and recovered nicely.

———••◉••———

Mikhail looked over to the elder healing Athie and smiled, sooty smoke coming out of his nostrils. When the elder was done with Athanasia's healing, he came back to Mikhail, saying, "You did a great job. I heard your agony. Was it extremely painful?"

"It was. I was not expecting that when my bones started contorting and resetting," Mikhail said in a voice much lower than his regular voice, "I've never felt anything like that before. Thankfully, it did not last long, and when I turned to this dragon form, all the pain was gone."

"I am glad it was only temporary. Are you good to go back to your half-dragon form, Mikhail?"

"If it is all the same to you, Elder Dionysios, I have wings. I want to fly!"

The elder nodded approval, and Mikhail was shocked again. Flying was just like walking for an adult. He just had to think to fly and he could do it. Mikhail had heard that dragon babies had the same experience, never having to learn to fly as birds did. He flew for hours, and when he returned, he crash-landed near their campsite as he was thoroughly exhausted.

Dionysios checked on him and suggested he turn back to his half-dragon form. Mikhail agreed, but when he did, he was not the same anymore. He was now something more, and yet, oddly something less than what he was before he transformed into a full obsidian dragon.

CHAPTER XVI

BATTLE BEGINS AT HOME

In their home, the Iroas family had a room for weapon practice. Here, the children were able to try a number of weapons and work on their proficiency using them. All of the children enjoyed archery. So, Nikodemos and Vhaidra, who were not archers, asked Miriam to train them in the skills of using bows and arrows at the monastery. Although they enjoyed archery, like their parents, this was not the top proficiency for any of the children.

Athie was best with an *urumi* sword, a scimitar, or a dagger. She tried to learn dual wielding of swords and scimitars, but could never get it down and would inadvertently hurt herself when trying. So, she eventually gave up. She could, however, wield one of the longer curved blades and also use a dagger at the same time with a lot of concentration. Vhaidra was able to teach her daughter from her own expertise in using a dagger, both as a ranged and melee weapon.

Damianos preferred great weapons and had his father teach him how to use a great sword like the paladins of The Way used, as he greatly admired them as heroes of his faith. Since Elder Dionysios had taught Nikodemos how to use a great sword, Nikodemos asked him to also teach Damianos as well. The elder would tie in the words of the scriptures of The Way to the moves of the great weapon, making it easier for the young half-drow to remember the moves needed with a large weapon like this.

———◆———

Kosmas enjoyed using hammers and throwing hatchets, but once he visited his best friend's father's blacksmith shop, he fell in love with the idea of carrying two dual-blade axes that could be thrown or used in close combat. Ti'erra taught him how to dance around attacks while using the axes since both axes and hammers were staples of the dwarven culture that she grew up in.

———◆———

It was one thing to learn how to use their weapons of choice, but they also needed to deal with attacks from other weapons, and as such, they would go against the teachers of the weapons other than those that they would be learning from when sparring. This helped them learn how to use their weapons, both offensively and defensively.

At the beginning and end of each session, Elder Dionysios would lead them in prayer, speaking of spiritual battles. Ti'erra's approach was different. She opened and closed each session with a hug and a kiss on the cheek. When the boys would kiss her back on her cheek, it always made her giggle. Every now and then, she would surprise one of them by arching back after transitioning from a regular hug to applying a bearhug, then suplexing them, teaching them to always be prepared for an attack from seemingly out of nowhere.

Nikodemos had wished that one of his children would have wanted to learn to use the Yan Yue Dao as he did. He even had one made for his daughter, but she never used it, nor did his sons. Because of this, he understood more the frustration his own father had when Nikodemos could not master the bow and arrow and used a crossbow instead in his youth.

Vhaidra, likewise, had hoped to teach one Crow or one of her siblings how to use the monastic weapons of the staff or the senior monk throwing daggers, but none seemed very interested after trying a few times. In fact, both weapons were extremely frustrating for the boys. Athanasia was able to use the dagger as a melee weapon, but just never got using it as a throwing weapon.

The couple was very happy to have friends that could teach their children the weapons that they loved and were proficient in using.

CHAPTER XVII

MORE HUMAN THAN HALF-HUMAN

Mikhail still turned to a humanoid form, going through a brief moment of intense pain as his wings contorted and merged back into his shoulder blades, but his face and hands looked a little more dragon-like and less human than before. He eventually realised that each time he transformed back from his draconic form, that he picked up more physical traits of a dragon. He wondered and hoped that eventually, he would have wings full-time. He liked the idea of this, as that was the most painful part of his transformation, and he would not miss this excruciating part of the change. While he looked more and more draconic, inside he felt even more human than before and less draconic.

YEAR 13

During another campout, Elder Dionysios had a vision that he talked to the Iroas family, Mikhail, and Ti'erra about.

"We are in a time of tranquillity and peace, but The Ancient of Days has allowed me to see that once these blessed children grow past the age of majority, a great darkness will come upon our city, nay, not only our city but our land and even the entire world. It is going to be a time of weeping and gnashing of teeth, and we may be thrust out of our city."

"Not again, Wizard!" Ti'erra replied, thinking about the year before the insane Battle of Sicyon.

"This time will be completely different. But I do not currently know much more than this. Please be on guard and be prepared for anything that may come in the coming years," warned the Elder.

"It sounds like it could be the last days!" Hypodiakonos Nikodemos replied.

"It could be, but I think it is just the birth pangs of the apocalypse, and not the actual apocalypse itself," Elder Dionysios explained, "I am sure that even worse things will come after my eventual repose."

"Let in not be so, Elder Dionysios!" Nikodemos cried out.

The news had quickly spread about Mikhail's ability to transform into an obsidian dragon, and he did not appreciate the extra attention, even when it came from one of the most beautiful high elven girls at school who were a few years younger than him.

Sometimes, when groups would gather around him and hound him with questions, he would transform into his dragon form and fly away to get away from all the enquirers. Unbeknownst to him, this made those very people that he was trying to get away even more excited about being around him and his awesome abilities. His desired reclusiveness helped make him long to be a monk, and preferably, a hermit. He knew that he was unlikely to be allowed to be a hermit when he first became a monk. So, he prayed that he would first be accepted into a skete, a monastery usually of four or less, and within a few years, could finally live out his hermitage desires and dreams.

He found that each time when he turned into his dragon form, he felt more draconic mentally, and when he changed back to his half-dragon form, he felt more human. Originally, he felt like he was an equal balance of both races in both forms.

YEAR 14

In the years before Mikhail turned fourteen, the dull grey scales he had where humans had hair slowly started turning into sharp glassy black scales that looked like obsidian. Once he was fourteen, since he was at the minimum age required to join a monastery, he requested to become a monk, not finding any female that he wished to court nor any other occupation that he desired to become an apprentice in. Episkopos Chrysostom readily agreed and gave him the black clothing of monasticism.

Elder Dionysios turned his catacomb hermitage into a skete of two monks to accept Mikhail, to ensure the novice monk could learn directly from him. He started learning the chants that could do the miraculous actions that his mentor could do, which the world called wizardry. Vhaidra altered his robes so that when he transformed into a dragon that his wings could come out without destroying them. Mikhail was exceptionally happy that he was in the skete when he started growing horns, as this would have caused even more excitement around him had he been out in the public like he was when he was in school.

YEAR 15

When he turned fifteen, Mikhail was given the belt and headgear of monasticism in addition to his black robes.

YEAR 16

At sixteen, he was given the neckwear of monks of The Way.

YEAR 17

At seventeen, Mikhail was given the armaments of monasticism, which for The Way, was a great schema like the one that Elder Dionysios wore. Since Mikhail was much taller than Elder Dionysios now, his great schema was much longer.

Mikhail's great schema was dark black and had bright white markings of the symbols of The Way, including spears, angels, skulls, and more. Conversely, Elder Dionysios' were now dark grey, and after the Battle for Sicyon against the Jet Fist Cult, where the white symbols were, they were now dark red, where they had absorbed the *living blood* created in that battle.

Around this same time, Archimandrite Olga had reposed, and Miriam, who had become a monk fourteen years ago, shortly after Athanasia was born, was named the new Archimandrite of the Transfiguration Cenobium by Episkopos Chrysostom. Her friends all joined at the elevation ceremony, happy for their friend to have become the lead monk of the monastery and orphanage that it ran.

After the service of elevation in monastic rank, the children went out to spend time with their friends who lived at the Orphanage of the Transfiguration Cenobium, while their parents attended a reception put on by the other female monastics of the Transfiguration Cenobium for their new archimandrite.

Miriam, who also now wore the great schema as a senior monk and archimandrite said to Vhaidra, Nikodemos, Ti'erra, and Elder Dionysios, "My friends, thank you for coming, but please pray for me as I pray for you. I have felt horrible demonic attacks ever since I decided to become a monk, especially from *Belial* and *Soneillon*. But now, I feel as if I am under even heavier attacks from the evil one, having been made an archimandrite."

Elder Dionysios replied, "We all pray for you every day. Every cleric, every monk, and every paladin feel attacks like these as they get closer to the Creator-Logos-Ghost and move up in rank. Keep yourself close to The Ancient of Days and in unceasing prayer, and he will protect you from the evil one."

After the reception, everyone took a blessing from the new archimandrite, kissing her hand in respect for her office.

———◆◆◆———

Elder Dionysios was shocked that almost immediately after receiving the great schema, Mikhail told him that The Ancient of Days had decreed that he would be a stylite, which is a hermit monk that lives atop a tower. Mikhail had already spoken to Episkopos Chrysostom and received his blessing to live on the tower on the temple mount in Sicyon. Dionysios prayed to the Creator-Logos-Ghost, confirmed that this was the destiny for Mikhail, and granted his blessing as well.

Mikhail loved the feeling of the sun on his scales, and really appreciated the heat of midday. Since his father came from the land of Erythraia, where the humans' skin was a brown so dark that it was almost black, Mikhail was a very dark-skinned half-human. Because his human skin was so dark, he did not have to worry about getting sunburned. Anywhere humans would have hair, Mikhail now had razor-sharp but shiny black scales, as his mother had been an obsidian dragon. In recent years, these scales covered most of his body and also much of his face, like a beard. He also had learned to control his power of breathing fire and to chant miraculous spells of the Way under the tutelage of Elder Dionysios, both while in his half-dragon and full dragon forms. His overall features looked more draconic than human every time he switched from dragon form back to half-dragon form. So, currently, his face, hands, and feet looked more draconic than human.

As an adult half-dragon, he could turn into an obsidian dragon at will, albeit one that was the same size that he was in half-dragon form, which was a little taller than average human size since he was currently six feet tall. He only required two hours of sleep per night, like his mentor, Elder Dionysios. So, late at night, when everyone was asleep, he would turn into his obsidian dragon form and fly high above the clouds, and then, patrol outside the city limits. This satiated his draconic desire for adventure and freedom from his self-imposed hermitage as a stylite and allowed him to be solely focused on his monastic studies and prayers during the day with no distractions. He felt like he truly had the best of both worlds now. However, he feared that, perhaps, one day, his two wills, the human and draconic wills, may be opposed to each other and, perhaps, battle with one another for dominance, driving him insane in the process. For now, he kept that fear to himself and focused even more intently on prayer.

CHAPTER XVIII

BLACK VS. WHITE

Mikhail had taken to the temple mount just in time. In fact, had it not been for long late-night patrols, Sicyon might have been ruined forever.

Late one night, as Mikhail was patrolling out over the nearby sea, he saw an unusual ship approach and open up to see a white dragon erupt from deep within the ship. Not only was this out of the ordinary, but oddly, the men on the boat were all tall and thick, and many of them had red beards. If his studies were correct, these were Varangians. He had thought that they had all settled and no longer were taking over lands, but that must have been wrong.

The white dragon headed right towards him and spoke in a language that Mikhail somehow understood, saying, "Oh, look, it is a little bitty black dragon! How quaint!"

"I am no simple black dragon; I am an obsidian dragon!" Mikhail replied.

Ormr was shocked that an obsidian dragon would be found here of all places.

"Who are you, and what is your kind doing here?"

"I am Mikhail. My friends and I protect this land."

"Obsidian dragons protecting the human race? Sounds unlikely!"

"We have a mutually beneficial relationship and mutual interests in protecting this place which is home to elves, dwarves, orcs, and humans living in peace!" Mikhail replied.

"How many of your kind are there?" the white dragon asked.

"Oh, I cannot even dare to count!" replied the obsidian dragon, not wishing to lie, but only to deceive.

"Hmm, well we will see about that."

Mikhail asked, "So, are you a crystal dragon?"

"No, I am the last white dragon, Ormr!"

"Oh, that is a pity, Ormr. No more white dragons will exist after you die?"

"I don't plan on dying anytime soon, obsidian soot!"

With that, Ormr the white dragon returned to the ship and spoke to the humans about what he learned. They decided to wait until daytime, and they would scout the town and see how many obsidian dragons that they could really see. Then, if they deemed it safe, they could have Ormr attack Sicyon at night.

———————

The next day, four men from the ship entered the town, each from one of the four cardinal directions. Mikhail saw this and approached each one individually, welcoming them to Sicyon, the home of obsidian dragon-kind. When they came to the middle of the town, where they met at the fountain, he swooped down, greeted them, pretending to have never met them, and welcoming them to Sicyon, the city of obsidian dragon encounters.

"How many obsidian dragons have you met so far?" Mikhail asked.

Each of them said they had only met one.

"That is rare that you would meet four other obsidian dragons other than me in Sicyon. Surely, you should stick around and see the unknowable number of mighty dragons that protect these lands!"

"We have only seen you five young obsidian dragons. Are there adult dragons in this city?"

"There may not be now, but soon, it shall be so," Mikhail replied, again craftily speaking the truth that one day he would be an adult dragon too.

The men were fearful of this and bid the dragon adieu, leaving town in a hurry. They waited on the shore a few miles away from Sicyon's port, where they had planned to meet their ship in the afternoon to report their findings to Asger, Ormr, and the other Varangians on the ship.

CHAPTER XIX

THE LONG-FROZEN WINTER

Mikhail reported what happened to Elder Dionysios, who then met at the Iroas home known as Omorfia Dipla Sto Potami. Vhaidra went and got Ti'erra to let her know about the threat.

Once they all were together, Elder Dionysios said, "Even though Mikhail has caused them to overestimate our abilities to defend Sicyon, we need to be ready for an attack from an adult white dragon."

Vhaidra complimented the half-dragon and said, "Great job with your deception of the Varangians, Mikhail! The four of us will just have to be attacking like dragons in a five-pronged attack if that did not scare them off."

Nikodemos added, "I guess that makes me the black dragon since my jade Yan Yue Dao does acid damage. Vhaidra is the green dragon since her daggers are poison-dipped. Elder Dionysios is the blue dragon since he can call down thunder and lightning. Ti'erra is *our* white dragon since she does frost damage, and of course, Mikhail is the obsidian dragon who can spit fire just like red dragons do."

"That is a problem, Cleric. I'm utterly useless in this battle," Ti'erra sighed.

"What is the problem?" Mikhail asked, even though Nikodemos was the one being spoken to.

"My greathammer will do no good against a white dragon. They are immune to freeze attacks! In fact, it will enjoy the freezing effect that my weapon gives, just like you would enjoy a fire or lava attack against you!"

"True," Mikhail admitted.

"Wrong!" Nikodemos added, "One, your hammer does more than frost damage, and two, you are not useless. You should be the one directing our attacks with a great strategy."

"Well, I guess I can do that, Cleric." Ti'erra smiled.

"Yes, Ti'erra should guide us from the temple mount and can use her hammer as necessary to create blunt force damage," Mikhail agreed.

"Okay, so let us come up with a plan quickly then. I am sure that they will attack tonight if they are still going to attack," Vhaidra said.

Then, they began planning the attack.

"That is what I would do if I were attacking us."

"Agreed, Monk." the dwelf replied.

The Varangians shared the information that they gained with Asger, who didn't like this change. As they discussed it, Ormr spoke up from underneath the hull.

"Let me make sure I understand this clearly. You saw five baby dragons and they said that the adult dragons would be returning soon?"

"Yes, Ormr," one of the Varangians explained.

"Then, why are we not attacking before the adults return? I can take on five wyrmlings without breaking a sweat," the white dragon said with a haughty laugh.

Asger replied, "If you think this is no problem, then we will act tonight."

"Why don't you just let me loose to freeze the town now?"

"If they see us release you in daylight, they may sink our boat while you attack!"

"Unlikely, but I will wait until dark, as you command, in order to save your short lives."

Ti'erra said that for their strategic planning, there might need to be sudden changes. So, she would use the correlating dragons that the cleric had mentioned earlier as codenames for them during the attack, as she yelled out commands from the temple mount in the middle of town. This way, the attacking white dragon would not know who its attackers were if it overheard her.

"Cleric, as you said, you are the black dragon. Monk, you are the green dragon..."

"That might be confusing since I am an obsidian dragon, and many people think that I am a black dragon," Mikhail once again interrupted.

"Please don't worry. You will have a different code name!"

"Oh, okay. I'll just wait and listen then," the half-dragon replied apologetically.

"I will be the white dragon, as the Cleric said. The Wizard will be the blue dragon, and our little Wizard Monk will be the red dragon since he breathes fire."

"I am hardly little, Ti'erra. I am taller than everyone in this room!" he explained, exasperated at being called little.

"True, but you are also the youngest, and in elven and dwarven culture, you are still just a baby!"

"Point taken, ma'am," he replied with resignation in his voice.

Nikodemos remarked, "Mikhail has a point about confusion. How will we know the difference when talking about you or the white dragon?"

"Oh, that is easy. We confuse it, in case it hears us. It will be the silver dragon!"

"Silver dragon? Why?" Nikodemos asked.

"Well, they have frost breath too. So, it fits."

"Works for me, Ti'erra!" Vhaidra replied with a smile.

"Let's go to the temple mount and scout out where we are going to defend our city."

"Good idea, but let me first go see Archon Justinian and let him know that the city is under a potential attack."

"That is wise," Elder Dionysios replied.

"Who will stay with the kids?" Ti'erra asked.

"They are now old enough to stay here, sleeping during the night in case anything happens. We'll just let them know that we'll be out, in case they wake up, so they won't be worried."

"Good idea, Monk. Let's head out to make our plan!"

The group headed out and figured out their strategic positions for an anticipated night-time attack. With the warning given to the Archon by Nikodemos, he had the city's guards standing by, mostly at the coast.

———◆◆◆———

This plan of attack worried the Varangians, but not Ormr. Once the cover of the night came, he would come out of the ship, far from the coast and catch the Sicyonites by surprise by flying close to the sea, while he froze them. He would give the city a long-frozen winter that they never expected in this temperate climate town!"

CHAPTER XX
ICE, ICE, BABY DRAGON

Ormr did exactly as he had said and surprised the guards on the beach, freezing many of them with his first breath of frost. Expecting a potential white dragon attack and being able to do something about it were two entirely different things for these city guards. The dragon still was hit by several arrows, but not enough to do any major damage.

"*Hmpf!* Just flesh wounds," Ormr huffed to himself.

Ti'erra was sad that those city guards lost their lives but glad that the dragon had expended one of its attacks on them, as it would take a while for it to recharge and be able to breathe a cone of frost again.

"Green dragon, black dragon, blue dragon, and red dragon, the silver dragon has been spotted!" she cried out in a loud voice from the temple mount.

Each of the so-called dragons was on top of a building, except for Elder Dionysios and Mikhail. The

Elder was near the temple but on the ground level, so he could hear strategic commands from Ti'erra while doing his chants.

As the dragon soared into the city, he thought to himself that the delays had hurt their chance of surprise, and now, these people knew that he was going to be attacking. He was somewhat lost in his thoughts as he heard a voice crying, "Now, green dragon, now!"

Vhaidra threw her poison-dipped daggers into its left wing. These small cuts hurt him more than the bows that had bitten him at the beach, as not only were they poison-dipped, but had mystical enchanted jacinth in them, which created a faerie fire that burned him. That caused him not only pain but made him angrier. As Ormr looked around for this assailant, he noticed that thunder clouds were starting to form overhead. It hadn't looked like rain was going to be coming in. So, Ormr found this very curious.

Thankfully Vhaidra was able to quickly hide after throwing her first volley of six daggers, and then, throw another volley, undetected by the giant beast flying towards the centre of the city.

Finally, the attack that he had expected came, as the fire hit his underbelly and gave him a lot of pain, making him lose concentration on building up a frost attack in his belly to spit out. He didn't see an obsidian dragon in front of him. So, he somersaulted, looping one hundred and eighty degrees and flew upside-down for a brief moment before he could twist to his normal position. This gave Vhaidra the chance to throw more daggers, this time, into its burned belly, and then, she obfuscated herself in the shadows once again.

Ormr howled in pain this time, as poison, cuts, and more burns on his already-burned belly hurt a lot. The amount of poison in each dagger was small in quantity in comparison to his size, but with his flesh already hurt, the pain just intensified. The white dragon was glad to see that one of the expected obsidian dragons was now just ahead of him, and he focused on building a belly full of freezing air to expectorate at the black wyrmling.

Ti'erra yelled out, "Now, blue dragon!"

Ormr heard it, but was trying to not be distracted by everything that was happening and only focused on preparing his attack on the obsidian gnat ahead. That concentration was broken as he heard a loud boom of thunder, and he was hit by many lightning strikes which grounded him just before he could breathe his cone of frost.

The next barked command was, "Black Dragon, attack!"

For a brief moment, this made Ormr wonder, because he had heard a cry for a dragon before he was hit by an attack of the element they breathed. *'Were there possibly other dragons protecting this town rather than the obsidian dragons?'* he wondered.

He wouldn't have much time to think, as suddenly, the rain started to pour down. Ormr felt a sharp pain of something coming down between his scales and into his flesh, causing acid damage at the base of his elongated neck. There was definitely something now attached to his back, causing him this serious pain. So, he tried to roll over on to his back to knock whatever it was off of his spine.

Hypodiakonos Nikodemos held on to his Yan Yue Dao with all his might as he was flipped around upside-down, holding himself close to the embedded blade, trying to prevent himself from being crushed by the dragon's immense form. Thankfully for him, the dragon would not be rolling around on his back for much longer!

With his belly one again exposed, Mikhail hit Ormr with another blast of fire, followed by another volley of daggers from Vhaidra, that caused fire and poison damage, along with more strikes of lightning from the thunderclouds that had been called by Elder Dionysios.

That caused the white dragon a lot more pain and anger. He decided to focus on the voice calling out the dragons instead. So, Ormr flipped around and flew towards the temple mount. He focused on building up his blast of frost from within his belly and told himself not to be distracted by the pain he felt, including the voices yelling at him and the thing lodged into his back.

As he approached Ti'erra, he heard a voice yell, "White dragon is in trouble. Red Dragon, evacuate the white dragon now!"

He saw this voice came from a small humanoid female, and he smiled as he billowed out a large cone of frost to freeze not only her but the entire temple whose tower she was standing on top of.

Just seconds before she was hit, she jumped from atop the temple mount. Ormr just laughed, thinking he wouldn't take any offence at her dying by suicide rather than his freezing blast. But he was, in fact, surprised when he saw that she landed on one of the baby black wyrmlings, which caused it to flutter as it glided to the ground into a crash, not being big enough to be a successfully mounted beast.

"Perfect!" Ormr said aloud to himself as he flew around the now-frozen temple, "Now, I can eat them both!"

When he went to bite at the small obsidian dragon, he was surprised that the little female humanoid was not there anymore. Not letting himself be bothered by this, he flew down, swallowing the obsidian wyrmling whole.

'Let him freeze in the belly!' Ormr thought to himself, while flying back to where the attacks of acid and fire had come from.

Mikhail screamed in fright, "NOOOOOOOOO!" as he tried his best to turn and slow his descent to the large dragon's belly from its long cavernous throat.

Ormr's prey never made it all the way down into his belly, however. As soon as he had swallowed the smaller black Wyrm, he felt the thing on his back go down deeper into him, separating his spine and the spinal cord that ran through it. That was the last thing he felt from that point at the base of his neck all the way to his long tail. Losing all feeling from that vertebrae down, caused him to stop flapping his wings, which lead to crashing and skidding along the road towards the harbour exit of the city, damaging buildings on the way. His legs and wings were now completely and utterly useless.

What the white dragon did not realise, was that Elder Dionysios had levitated Ti'erra back into the air and dropped her so that she could use her greathammer to drive Nikodemos' Yan Yue Dao into and through the dragon's spinal cord.

Inside Ormr's throat, Mikhail spit out a huge fireball towards the belly of the white dragon. Which caused the Wyrm to regurgitate its prey into a frozen bile slush on the street ahead of it.

⁕⬤⁕

One of the buildings that had been hit by the crashing white dragon belonged to the duergar master blacksmith TaeLyon. The *duergars* or *grey dwarves* had dark grey skin and white hair just like the dark elves. Most people did not trust them, but they prized the powerful weapons they created. No other race made such fine weapons.

TaeLyon was a member of The Way, but he rarely attended the divine services, as he was always busy in his shop, creating the best weapons that one could desire. After checking on his family members, he ran out of his combined home and shoppe, only wearing his skivvies and asking what was happening.

"TaeLyon, this white dragon attacked our city and we have grounded it, but my weapon is stuck deep in its spine!" Nikodemos explained.

"I guess you will be in the market for one of my fine weapons then!" smiled the grey dwarf.

"Well, not actually. I was hoping that I could borrow one of your greataxes to cut it out!"

"Borrow? Never! Buy? Yes! That will cost you quite a lot of gold, Chosen of The Ancient of Days!"

"Would you take the white dragon scale for armour instead?"

TaeLyon replied, "Hmmm, I like your thinking! It is a deal."

Nikodemos grabbed the greataxe, but before he could even use it, he found that Ti'erra had stolen it away from him and was doing a dance with it as she approached the dragon.

"That dwelf sure is one amazing dancer, isn't she?" TaeLyon asked the hypodiakonos.

"She sure is, TaeLyon, but she's an even better tactician. If not for her, we surely would not have felled this large beast tonight!"

"Then, Sicyon is doubly lucky to have her amongst its residents."

"Indeed, we are, master blacksmith. Indeed, we truly are."

Together, the human cleric and the duergar blacksmith watched Ti'erra do one of her seductive dances as she prepared to put the final blow on the downed beast. Likewise, all that were awakened in the area by the crashing Dragon did the same.

CHAPTER XXI

DRACONIC AFTERMATH

"I'm not dead yet!" roared Ormr, trying to build up a frost in his belly, but found himself unable to, as he had no feeling below his lower neck. He was also feeling quite woozy from the injuries and poison throughout his body.

Ormr started biting the road ahead of him, dragging his limp body from behind him, but as he started to do so, he noticed that the surviving city guards were heading his way from the beach, which was his destination. Also, there was a dazed and injured young obsidian dragon in a pile of frozen bile ahead as well.

Ormr knew he was likely to die, and unfortunately, there was nothing he could do about it. In retrospect, he had been too arrogant like most dragons naturally were. He kept biting the road, pulling himself towards the water that seemed to be miles away, until he felt a great axe cut his neck open, gushing his life-sustaining blood over all the dwelf that had sliced him open. That was the last thing he ever felt, as his head slumped to the road and he gave up this mortal coil.

After she completed her dance around the dead dragon, Ti'erra exclaimed, "Thanks, Blacksmith!" She then added with a hearty laugh, "That is one very sharp greataxe!"

"I only make the sharpest and most perfectly-weighted weapons!" TaeLyon replied with a snooty tone. "If you ever need to replace your enchanted dwarven greathammer, you know where to come!"

Ti'erra smiled at TaeLyon and walked over to Nikodemos, her body and armour now completely covered in blood. She said, "Here you go, Cleric. Now, you can cut out your Yan Yue Dao!"

The hypodiakonos smiled and did as she suggested. He retrieved his weapon after quite a few mighty blows. After he was completed with the task at hand, he limped over and returned the greataxe to TaeLyon, who had started skinning the dragon so that he could make dragon scale armour from it.

"No need to return it to me now, Nikodemos. I figure you have purchased it, as I will be able to sell many suits of white dragon scale armour from this fine specimen."

"Thank you, master blacksmith! I understand why my youngest son speaks so highly of your weapons!"

"As he should. Your son has a fine eye for quality and detail obviously! No wonder he is best friends with my son, Hemet! Perhaps, one day, I can bring him on as an apprentice?"

"I think he would enjoy that even more than you would, master blacksmith!"

"Never underestimate the value that a blacksmith puts on young, strong, and most importantly, free labour!" he responded with a snorting laugh.

"Well, that was disappointing!" Vhaidra huffed to Ti'erra.

"What was disappointing, Monk?"

"I never even had a chance to call upon Skeletogre."

"Well, not all battles happen in the way we plan them. I'm just glad that we not only survived but won!"

"I guess so, but..."

"But nothing, Monk! I don't think he would have been very effective, to be honest, and it just made for one less person to keep track of as our strategist!"

"I guess you are right, Ti'erra."

"Plus, you do not always need him in battle. You are fierce and deadly as anyone I know!"

"Me? Look at you. You are literally covered from head to toe in dragon blood. I have to say that you were the fiercest instrument of death in this battle."

Ti'erra playfully licked the dragon blood off her fingers and laughed, "Mmmm, delicious! The sweet, sweet taste of victory!"

"Are you sure you are not part drow or duergar?" Vhaidra joked with her best friend.

"Ha! I'm just a vicious golden wood dwelf!"

Mikhail was injured from his crash landing that had saved Ti'erra as well as from being swallowed whole and then disgorged by the white dragon. He was now drinking some healing potions and having prayers chanted by Elder Dionysios. Suddenly, the Elder stopped and asked Mikhail to change back to his half-dragon form.

"Why, Elder?"

"I have a hypothesis and want to check to see if it is correct."

"Can we do it after I heal?"

"No, it is important that we do it before you heal completely."

"Okay, Elder, here we go."

Mikhail chugged the last of the healing potion and went through the painful transformation, converting back to his more human form, looking a little more draconic than he had the last time he was in this form.

"Interesting! I was correct!"

"What were you correct about, Elder?"

"Do you feel any pain?

"No! Wow! Why?"

"Apparently, your injuries only continue as long as you are in that form. Once you switch, the injuries disappear."

"Why?"

"That, Mikhail, I do not know yet. Perhaps, we can have an apothecary from the Noskomeio investigate it more."

"I'd rather not be poked and prodded by these people who just see me as a monster, if it is all the same to you, Elder."

"I understand completely, Mikhail. I will not require this of you at all."

"Thank you, Elder!"

With that, Mikhail changed back to his dragon form and was shocked that he was fully healed in this form too. This was very advantageous for him, as if he was ever seriously injured in one form, he could switch to the other and then back, being back to normal in a matter of minutes! Thinking over the possibilities of this feat, he flew up to the temple mount and started using his fire to thaw out the temple which had been hit when Ormr attacked Ti'erra.

The uninjured city soldiers took the injured troops to the Noskomeio, a place for healing the sick and dying. The Noskomeio was what Archon Justinian had used Nikodemos' land to build after the Battle of Sicyon, where so many were injured due to the actions of the Jet Fist Cult. He had anticipated a place may be needed in the future for healing many, and he had been correct.

TaeLyon called over Ti'erra after she was done talking with Vhaidra and asked, "Have you heard about what has been happening with some of the wood elves not too far from here?"

"No, I have not, blacksmith."

"Well, I hear that some of them started getting really sick. Some kind of fey plague or something."

"Oh, that is too bad. How did you hear about this?"

"There are some wood elves who go on adventures with the parents of one of the high elves at the local school. They came into the shop and were talking about it. I'm surprised you don't know; don't you have wood elven kin?"

"I do, but I don't regularly communicate with them. Still, I am saddened about this."

"Let me know if you hear anything more," TaeLyon added.

"Sure thing!" Ti'erra replied and browsed through TaeLyon's smithy shop while the blacksmith skinned the dragon outside.

Unbeknown to the dwelf dancer, TaeLyon's wife was secretly watching her and taking note of what items she browsed through and appeared to have an interest in.

Vhaidra checked on Nikodemos and saw that he had a bit of a limp.

"Hypo, how badly are you injured?"

"Not too badly. I am more jostled than anything, dear."

"I'm glad to hear that. Let's go home."

"Sure; but let me first make a full report to the archon. He needs to know what happened here."

"Okay, but come home as soon as you are done. I don't want our children to be worried in case the noises of the battles worried them."

"I'll be back as quickly as I can!" he said to his wife with a smile and a kiss.

"Nikodemos, thank you for the report," Archon Justinian said, "I am glad that you and your team were able to save our fair city yet again."

"Well, to be fair, your city guard archers gave the white dragon its first injuries, and they were running in to finish the job when the dragon was finally killed. They were brave and strong. May the memory of those who died be eternal."

"Amin! I still cannot believe that that little dwelf dancer gave the dragon its final blows, both in the air and on the ground!"

"Ti'erra is quite a strategist and an important part of our team. I daresay many of our battles would have ended in defeat if it were not for her."

"Then, I am glad that she is on our side, Nikodemos. Please return home and send your family and friends my deepest regards on behalf of our entire city."

"Yes sire," Nikodemos replied, bowing towards the Archon of Sicyon.

Nikodemos did exactly as the archon suggested. He went back to his home of Omorfia Dipla Sto Potami and awaited the return of the others so that they could debrief.

But first, he was going to have to answer to his children.

CHAPTER XXII
COUNTING CROWS

Athie had awoken from her slumber during the battle raging near the city centre. One of her calling crows stood at her window, cawing for her to retrieve the message attached to its foot.

The message was shocking to Athie. It was so shocking that she read it aloud to make sure her sleepy mind understood it.

"Dear Athie,

We have enjoyed corresponding with you. You are now of age, and we wish to get to know you even better. Our group of half and full-blooded high, wood, and dark elves would like for you to come to visit us as you strike your own path of adulthood. Attached is a map, showing you the safest way to come and meet us. Please do not delay, as we long to see you in person soon.

Dance and be blessed,

Priestess Vierae Auvryval"

'*Oh, Father will not like this at all,*' she thought to herself. Athie figured her mother would give her blessing, but the Chosen of The Ancient of Days was so protective of his only daughter, that it would be a struggle convincing him to let her go. Especially, if he knew she was going to visit a community with a drow priestess. She decided right then and there that she would leave this part out once she gained the courage to tell her parents that she was ready to strike out on her own and travel the world.

"Athie, did you hear what Mom and Dad did?" Damianos cried out.

"No, what happened?"

"You didn't hear all the sounds?"

"Sorry, I have been really focused on this message from one of my calling crows."

"Oh, what did it say?"

"Oh, never you mind, Damianos. What did Mother and Father do?"

"They fought a dragon with Ti'erra, Elder Dionysios, and Mikhail!"

"What? They let Mikhail help them fight off a dragon?"

"I know, right? They should have let us help too!"

"Damianos, I know we have all been trained in the use of weapons since we were little, but you haven't even joined, let alone graduated your paladin school yet. There will be plenty of chances to fight after you are done with your advanced studies and training."

"But, Athie, it was a white dragon, and it claimed it was the last one! A chance to kill the last white dragon. How amazing is that?"

"Pretty amazing, I guess!"

All of a sudden, Kosmas came crashing into Athie's room, fully armoured and wielding twin battleaxes, saying, "I'm ready, let's go to battle!"

"Too late, Kosmas. Mom just came home, and they already defeated the dragon."

"There was a dragon?" Kosmas asked.

"Yes, they downed it over by TaeLyon's shoppe!"

"Oh, then I am going to go check on it then!" and he turned around and ran out Athie's doorway, only to crash into his father and knock him down.

"Dad, I'm so sorry. I was going to go see the dragon!"

Nikodemos replied, "There will be plenty of time for…"

"Dad, why didn't you tell us? We wanted to help kill the last white dragon!" Damianos asked.

"One day, you may join us in battle, but not today, and especially, not against as fierce a foe as a white dragon!"

"But, Dad, you've trained us since we were little. We were ready for this!"

Nikodemos walked up to his oldest son, spun him around, pinned his arms behind his back and gently tossed him to the ground, saying, "Not today, Damianos, but one day."

Athie laughed and added, "I told you that you would not be ready until after you graduate paladin school."

Nikodemos was going to add to that but was called away by his wife, as the party was going to debrief, seeing what worked well, what did not, and what they could do to improve in the future.

CHAPTER XXIII

ANIMUS OF THE ARCHIMANDRITE

Archimandrite Miriam had heard of what happened, and at the first light of morning, she had sent one of her monks to call upon Elder Dionysios, Mikhail, Hypodiakonos Nikodemos, Vhaidra, and Ti'erra to come to the monastery immediately.

"I heard a dragon attacked Sicyon last night and almost destroyed our temple?"

"Mother Miriam, it wasn't me."

"Of course, Mikhail, I know that. It was a white dragon, I heard."

"Yes, it was, Ranger. 'Tis a pity that you were not able to join us for the battle. We could have used your marksmanship and ranged attack skills!" Ti'erra explained.

"Those days are long behind me, Ti'erra. I was part of your party for a few more battles than I would have liked," Miriam said with a sour face.

"What do you mean?" Vhaidra asked.

"Well, it seems that your journeys were constantly full of battles. Do you think that there is any chance that your notoriety could possibly attract enemies to you?"

"I think that is kind of farfetched," Nikodemos replied.

"Are you sure? After all, didn't you say that Episkopos Andrew of Rakote said this of your party? Are you so quick to dismiss the words of a spiritual father of The Way?"

The hypodiakonos considered it, saying, "*Hmmm.*"

"To be fair, Ranger, at that time, we had the Black Fist Cult chasing us because this party had freed me from slavery."

"Yet, did not Hypodiakonos Nikodemos and Vhaidra cause a cyclops to attack an inn in Corinth, destroying it? Did not this same cleric's presence cause the death of a doctor in Lechaeum and a drow in the forests near there? Did not a copper dragon attack innocent because of all of you in Rakote? Was it not your cause that an obsidian dragon destroyed yet another inn in Rakote as well? Quite honestly, it seems like you are a magnet for trouble!"

"Archimandrite Miriam, before this attack, there had not been any such problems since the Battle for Sicyon."

"True, but I don't want this to become the new normal like it was for you before. You know that the people of Sicyon have a hard time trusting other races already. If our resident drow, dwelf, half-orc, and obsidian dragon were thought to be magnets for trouble, well, I would hate to see what would occur."

"I assure you that we have no intent on being a beacon for troubles," the Elder explained.

"Mother Miriam, we killed the dragon, and in talking to him, he claimed he was the last white dragon. Also, the people with him seemed to be Varangians – people from very far away."

"Varangians?"

"They are a nomadic people from the great white north, and they are known for attacking lands that they want to take over for their empire. If they have targeted Sicyon, their target is much more than five or six adventurers."

"I hope you have shared this with Archon Justinian then."

"Not yet, but Elder Dionysios and I planned to request an audience with him today after debriefing with the team last night, Mother Miriam."

Hypodiakonos Nikodemos added, "I actually met with him late last night, and he was very happy with the defence that we gave the city. And he was quite impressed with Ti'erra's actions in the fight!"

"Really, Cleric?" the dwelf asked.

"Yes. He appreciated both your tactics and your final blows on the Wyrm."

"Yay!" Ti'erra squealed with delight.

"Anyway, that is all. I just wanted to ensure that this was not going to be a regular thing and wanted to warn you to make sure that this does not become our new normal."

"It won't be," Elder Dionysios added, "In fact, without Mikhail being on the tower of the temple mount, we would have never known about this attack and would not have been prepared for it. Likewise, if not for him, the temple would be frozen in a solid brick of ice."

"Very well. Good job, Mikhail."

Mikhail smiled and asked for her blessing as they departed. Everyone else followed suit.

———•◦●◦•———

"Well, that was very odd, don't you think?" Nikodemos asked the Elder once they were outside the monastery's gates.

"Indeed, I am afraid that the demonic attacks she spoke of when she became an archimandrite are increasing. We should redouble our prayers for her. For some reason, she appears to be living in fear of what is coming next."

"But, Wizard, didn't you say you had a premonition that something bad would happen in Sicyon?"

"That was probably just the attack of the white dragon," Vhaidra answered before Dionysios could reply.

"No, Vhaidra. While I could not say anything in front of Miriam, I fear something much worse is coming in the not too distant future. Something completely different that will entirely overshadow this attack we dealt with."

"Wizard, what will it be?"

"I am not sure, but as I said before, it is going to be a time of weeping and gnashing of teeth, and we may be thrust out of our city before it is completed."

"Such a fearful forecast, Wizard."

"But let us not take Miriam's warnings as a negative. Let us do our best to earn goodwill and build up this city. In order to do that, I suggest we go to the archon and talk to him immediately."

"Everyone, Elder?"

"Yes, Mikhail. We should all go, I think."

"Then let's do this thing!" Ti'erra shouted with glee.

———◆———

Unbeknownst to the party, Miriam had one of her monks nearby, recording what was being said on a piece of parchment. She reported back to Miriam and told her everything that they had said when they thought that they had been confidential between themselves.

"Just as I thought. Something on an apocalyptic level is coming and soon. I knew I sensed something."

Miriam then turned to the monk who had acted as a spy and a scribe to get this information, "Let your fellow monks know that our archery practice is to be increased immediately. Not only for us but the children as well. We will be ready to defend the monastery and orphanage from the evils that dare wage a savage attack on us!"

"Yes, as you command, Archimandrite Miriam," she said, bowing and running off to tell the others.

CHAPTER XXIV

THE SONS OF BELIAL

Unfortunately, the archon was busy. Instead, they had to leave a message with his assistant, *Lev Kakoi*, letting him know about the Varangians and the white dragon claiming to be the last of his kind. Elder Dionysios also shared his intuition that much worse was coming for Sicyon.

Unfortunately for them, the assistant did not trust them and threw away the notes after the party had left. So, the archon would never get the warning or important information about the attackers that had come to their city.

The way that Lev thought about it was that even if something happened, it, at worst, would discredit Archon Justinian, and then, he could take over as Archon of Sicyon as he felt that he should be. Besides that, he hated elves, half-elves, or any half-race creature. He would not allow this half breeds and elven folk to be the heroes of this town again.

He knew he was not alone in these feelings. So, he wrote a letter, requesting that Archon Justinian give awards to the human father of half-drow, the drow, the dwelf, the half-orc, and the half-dragon. When the time of troubles came, he would ensure that they were blamed, and Archon Justinian would be associated in the public eye with these reprobates.

That night, Lev called together his supporters, the secret society called the *Sons of Belial,* to their surreptitious underground headquarters, where all of the men stood in a circle. Inside the circle of human males was a hexacle carved into the stone floor that was stained with old, dried blood and had candles lit at each point where the various lines intersected. He let them know that he had received information that something bad was going to come upon the city and that this was the moment that they had been waiting for. They would let Archon Justinian fall, and Lev would take over. It would allow all of their supporters to get positions of power and prestige.

"Belial be praised!" he shouted.

"Belial be praised!" the replied in unison as Lev grabbed his ceremonial knife and stabbed his wrist, letting the blood pour onto the hexacle on the floor. He handed the knife to the man on his left and he did the same thing until every man present had extravasated onto the pentacle.

Their blood came together in the middle of a hexacle, and when it did, their candles all went out, making it pitch black. The hexacle began to glow with wild magicks, and raised off the ground to the eye level of the men encircled about it. They then heard an evil voice chanting the following words:

"My sons, my time is near,

Spill more blood and bring on fear

Divide the populace make them abate,

Kill them all that you may hate,

Desire the good things for you alone,

And make all of my enemies atone.

Sacrifice is what I require,

Ensure the days ahead are dire,

We'll poison the air, the earth, the sea,

We'll fill their hearts with every vile thing,

Make them want until they can want no more,

Then blame their lack on the one next door,

When hate grows stronger, so will I,

As they take tooth for tooth and eye for an eye!"

After that was said, the hexacle appeared to drop to the floor causing an impact so powerful that the men were thrown against the walls of their subterranean base of operations. The candles lit again, but this time, the fire was red, and the huge flames danced strangely in large figures, jumping from one candle to the next.

"Who will sacrifice himself for Belial?" Lev asked.

One man, seemingly in a trance, walked to the middle of the hexacle, and said, "I, Gleb, offer myself to Belial willingly and purposely!"

As he said the words, the giant red flames danced from the candles to his body, shredding him to nothingness.

"May the chaos of *anomie* come soon!" Lev cried out.

"*Synnomie* to anomie, good to evil, order to chaos, from others to Belial!" the society chanted back in response to Lev's cry for anomie.

CHAPTER XXV

ENTER THE WARLOCK

Asger had stayed up all night, waiting for the return of Ormr, the white dragon. When the sun came up and he did not see him, he became worried. He ordered the Varangians to take the ship to shore.

"In broad daylight, sir?"

"Yes, we must see what is delaying Ormr."

"Aye, sir!" the men replied and started rowing for the shore.

***

In the midday, a tall, bearded human came up to the duergar that was taking the skin and scales off the defeated white dragon. He greeted the master blacksmith saying, "Hello, TaeLyon!"

"Oh, Archon Justinian! Whatsoever reason do I have the pleasure of your presence?" the duergar asked.

"Well, you are skinning a dragon on a city road, and this dragon is blocking the way."

"Yes, sir. Hypodiakonos Nikodemos granted me this dragon's skin so that I can make some fine white dragon scale armour for the brave men and women of this fine city!"

"Indeed, that is what he tells me. I would like to order a suit of this armour for each of my city guards so that they cannot be frozen, should another such attack be happening again."

"Oh, that would be quite expensive sir."

"Exactly how expensive would it be, TaeLyon?"

"Well, dragon scale mail sells usually for about one thousand two hundred gold pieces a suit. But I could give you a discount, charging you only nine hundred gold pieces per suit."

"I have a better idea, TaeLyon. How about I exempt your shop from taxes, and you give them to me for only six hundred gold pieces apiece. After all, your material cost for the scales is free!"

"Yes, but it is still a lot of work. I will have to work sixteen hours a day and add another apprentice to my shop in addition to my twins!"

"But you will be known as the armourer of the city guards. Surely that will drive more business to you."

"Only if I am the exclusive weapon and armour provider of the city government, my archon."

"Hmm, you drive a hard bargain, but if you will give them up for five hundred gold pieces each and we get all of them, I will sign a ten-year contract, making you the exclusive armourer and weapon provider to the city government and exempt you from all taxes for that time."

"It's a deal, Archon Justinian! I'll have my wife draw up the contracts," TaeLyon said, reaching out to shake his hand, but the archon instead handed him a contract with the terms of the deals that they had just agreed upon.

"How...how...how is this possible?"

"I figured that there were a few possibilities on how these discussions would go. So, I had a few different options written up so that we could get the contract signed, sealed, and delivered as quickly as possible."

"You are wise beyond your years, Archon Justinian. I guess I'll just sign here...," and TaeLyon did as he said he would do, signing an exclusive contract with the city to be the weaponeer and armourer for the government.

⸺⋅•●•⋅⸺

Asger, the warlock, told his men after dropping him off on the seashore to take the ship back into the middle of the gulf that they were in and to let him go investigate what was delaying their dragon. They obediently did as they were told. The warlock saw only a few chunks of ice remaining as the dead soldiers had been chipped away from frozen blocks. This made him smile. What did not make him smile was walking down the street and seeing his dragon dead on the road and a grey dwarf skinning him. He ran up to the duergar and asked him what had happened.

"What happened to this white dragon? Why are you skinning it?"

"Hello, stranger. I am TaeLyon, the master smith of this here blacksmith shoppe, and I am creating dragon scale armour for the fine men and women of Sicyon. As far as what happened to this dragon...well, he chose the wrong city to attack. We are a city with some fierce protectors, one of whom is the chosen of our god!"

"Oh my! I am Asger. Was it one of your famous dragons who killed it?"

TaeLyon said with a laugh, "I guess one might say that Qing Long, the green dragon downed him, but it was our giant tortoise..."

Asger interrupted TaeLyon before he could finish describing Ti'erra and said, "Green dragon? I thought this was the city of obsidian dragons?"

"Oh, we have one of those too. You can see him up on the top of the temple mount" he replied, pointing to the Temple of The Way just beyond the city centre.

"That? That looks like just a wyrmling."

"That he may be, but he is our wyrmling."

"May I look around in your shoppe?"

"Of course, just let me know if there is anything that you like. I need to get this skin off before he starts to rot."

"What will you do with the meat?"

"Oh, he is full of acid and poison now. So, that meat is no good for consumption anymore. I imagine his carcass will just be drug out to sea where sea creatures can eat him."

"And die?"

"Something big likely won't die from the poison like something small such as we would."

"That makes sense. I guess I'll go look around."

"Please do!"

After a while, Asger came out with an axe and shield, complimenting TaeLyon on its sturdy and balanced construction. He paid the duergar. As he left, he hit the dragon with his new axe and pulled out an almost empty vial to collect its blood, secretly taking a solitary scale as well. The vial was empty, save for a drop of a mana potion, a drop of a freezing potion, and a drop of a healing potion.

"What are you doing?" TaeLyon asked.

"Well, since you said there were no plans for anything but the scales, I wanted to take a sample of its blood for study."

"Very well. Suit yourself then. Please come again!"

"Oh, I will. I definitely will, and bring others with me," Asger said with a sneer on his face.

"I'll look forward to your return then. Good day!"

The warlock walked back to the beach, looked at the vial of blood that he had, and whispered to no one in particular, "Ormr, you may have failed us, but with your blood, I can create you again, and this time, you will succeed in your mission!"

He then shot a bolt above the ship that was waiting for him, giving them the signal that it was time to come pick him up.

The men on the boat were saddened. If Asger wasn't returning on the white dragon, that probably meant that Ormr was dead. Their king would not be happy about this outcome at all. He had big plans for this land.

Asger took a drop of the seawater and added to his vial with the blood. He also took the small dragon scale and placed it in the vial. He then plucked a beard hair and put it in the container. Then Asger cut his finger with the axe and added his own blood. Lastly, he took a little mud from the seashore and placed it in the glass container.

He chanted the following enchantment spell,

"Bloot ork skales,

Harr ork bloot,

Fran andlac pu leaf,

Ork inn I einn ess pu becamc,

Servancr or minn,

Minn drason servanc!"

He then threw the vial on a sharp rock. The rock exploded and then imploded, changing into an off-white egg with faint green spots on it, causing Asger to laugh with a vile cackle.

"Yes, Ormr dies, but he will live again, and this time, he will not fail!"

With that completed, he picked up the heavy egg and started walking into the sea, not even waiting for his ship to arrive. He walked on the sea just as if it was dry land.

Elsewhere, TaeLyon was shocked as all of the blood that had poured out of the white dragon that he had been skinning suddenly disappeared. He could sense that some evil magic was in play. He immediately thought back to Asger and knew that it would not be the last time that they would meet.

He stopped what he was doing, wrote down everything that he could remember of his encounter with the Varangian warlock, and had his wife deliver it to the Archon of Sicyon.

TaeLyon was not the only one to have something unusual happen related to the blood of Ormr the white dragon. Ti'erra, who had been coated in the dragon's blood and had playfully licked a blood-covered finger, suddenly felt as if she had been punched deep in her stomach. In fact, it had hit her so hard and so suddenly as she danced that she fell from her greathammer that she was spinning on and curled into a fetal position. The tavern owner had one of the bouncers, an orc named Rokmaw, run her over to the Noskomeio immediately.

CHAPTER XXVI

PARALYSED BY THE BLOOD OF ORMR

Mikhail saw Rokmaw running to the Noskomeio with Ti'erra. So, Mikhail went to Elder Dionysios to tell him what had happened. Dionysios sent him to alert Vhaidra and Nikodemos to pray for her.

Ti'erra had everything exit her intestines from both ends all over Rokmaw the Orc bouncer as he ran her to the Noskomeio. Once they arrived, the orc was instructed to lay Ti'erra on a bed in one of the vacant rooms. In a short amount of time, the Noskomeio's lone doctor and an apothecary came to check on the dwelf.

"Doctor Nurah, this is a dwelf. She is half sylvan and half gold dwarf," the apothecary, Maibrar said to her fellow female high elf.

"Yes, this is true, but first let's see what ails her."

"Of course, doctor."

The orc explained that Ti'erra was a dancer and that she was in the middle of dancing when she fell, curled up in the fetal position, and was knocked unconscious. He ran her over here immediately, and she had vomited and had diarrhoea all over him.

"Well that explains the smell then," the apothecary explained.

"Yes, is she going to be okay?" Rokmaw asked.

"We will do our best," the doctor replied.

Rokmaw asked, "Do you have someplace that I can clean up?"

"Yes, we will have a nurse show you the way. She will probably be with us for a few days. So, please let the tavern owner know that she is in good hands."

"I will, thank you."

Doctor Nurah called for a nurse. A human female with waist-length curly blonde hair entered the room and led the orc bouncer to another floor to get cleaned up. They let the nurse know to collect samples of the vomit and diarrhoea for testing purposes while the orc bathed.

"A domesticated orc?" Maibrar commented.

"Yes, that is not as unusual as you would think. There was a cleric of The Way named Romanos that once made content a group of orcs and had them join The Way. In fact, a number of females even became monks and joined a monastery. That man had a gnome for an assistant that rode on a domesticated wolf too. It was amazing the work he did in racial harmony amongst races that were so often in enmity with one another!"

"That is something to study for your future plans."

"Indeed, it is, but let us get back to our patient."

When they looked down at Ti'erra they found her stirring, asking, "Where am I?"

"Hello, Ti'erra, I am Doctor Nurah, and this is Apothecary Maibrar. You are at the Noskomeio, and we are going to find out what is wrong with you."

"You ladies are high elves?" she asked.

"Yes, yes, we are. Is that a problem?"

"No, no. I was just shocked. I didn't realise the new doctor was an elf. I'm glad to hear it. How did I get here? What happened?"

"An orc bouncer from The Pink Wyrm brought you here. He said you fell off the top of your dancing pole, curled up into the fetal position, and passed out."

"Oh yeah, I remember an intense pain from my bowels, and then, that was it. Then, I awoke here."

Just then, Elder Dionysios ran into the room, out of breath, and asked, "Is Ti'erra here? Is she okay?"

The dwelf asked, "Wizard, is that you?"

The apothecary turned around and said, "Sorry, sir. We are checking on the patient right now. We need you to wait outside. You may visit her after we are done here."

"Is she okay?"

"She will be if you allow us to help her."

"Okay, I will wait outside and begin prayers for her."

"Thank you, Wizard!" Ti'erra explained, sounding quite happy that he was there.

"So, Ti'erra, have you eaten anything unusual recently?"

"Hmm, nothing that I can think of really...." she began, and then, added, "Well, I did swallow some dragon blood."

The apothecary excitedly asked, "Dragon blood? Aren't you a follower of The Way that forbids drinking blood?"

"One, no I am not a member of The Way, and two, yes, dragon blood."

"Okay, how much did you ingest?" the doctor asked.

"I was covered in dragon blood, and I sucked all the blood off of one or two of my fingers," replied the dwelf, matter-of-the-factly.

"So, monster blood. How long had the animal been dead before you did this?"

"Maybe a few minutes at most."

"Did you cook it before you ingested it?"

"No, it had poured right out of the dragon's neck, all over me when I sliced its throat."

"Hmm, so maybe draconic digestive juices were present as well?"

"Oh, and the dragon had thrown up right before I killed it if that helps anyway."

"Good information!" we are going to take the sample of your blood, vomit, and diarrhoea and run some tests. Are you feeling any better now?

"Not one hundred per cent, but yes, much better than when I first fell ill!"

The apothecary added, "This might hurt just a little," as he pulled out a dagger and pricked Ti'erra's thumb, collecting a sample of her blood in a vial. After she was done collecting it, she wrapped up her thumb with some hemp cloth.

After the wound was wrapped, she said, "We'll be back soon."

The doctor and the apothecary left, and then, Elder Dionysios came in, now escorted by Vhaidra, Hypodiakonos Nikodemos, and Mikhail.

She smiled and was so happy to see all of her friends in her hospital room.

"Are you okay?" Vhaidra asked, "What happened?"

Nikodemos handed her a healing potion mixed with holy water and anointed her with holy oil on her forehead, eyelids, ears, nose, lips, belly, back, hands, and feet in the shape of the holy symbol of The Way which was one large circle with four smaller but equal-sized circles the width of the circle's radius inside it.

Mikhail stood at Ti'erra's feet and started chanting for healing, the same thing that Elder Dionysios had done while waiting for the doctor and apothecary to leave.

Ti'erra explained what happened, and then, that the doctors were going to test the fluids that she had projected out of her body after the pain had hit her.

Nikodemos then tied a crown of blessed holy basil around her head and quietly said a prayer of healing as well.

Vhaidra pleaded with her best friend, "Ti'erra, please never drink dragon blood again! It sounds like they suspect this caused your illness!"

"I guess I will leave that to drow and duergar, Monk!" she joked.

Ti'erra started feeling better after drinking the holy water and healing potion and being anointed with holy oil and blessed basil. She was sure that the prayers had helped as well.

Mikhail asked Ti'erra, "I hope that you do not mind that I let Mother Miriam know as well."

"Of course, not. Why would I mind?"

"I know she came off as somewhat xenophobic the last time we met with her."

"We used to live together; I adore the Ranger. I'm glad you let her know!"

"Good. She has her entire monastery praying for you right now."

"That is very kind of her," Ti'erra smiled and then yawned. "Oh, I am suddenly very tired. I think I am going to go to sleep."

"I'm sure you deserve a nice nap. We'll leave you to your rest."

"Thank you, my friends, I am the luckiest dwelf in the world to have friends like you all!"

Elder Dionysios walked over, grabbed her hand, and patted it with his other hand, smiling. That gave Ti'erra a surprised smile. She winked at the Elder, and then, dozed off shortly after he left her room.

Shortly after her friends left, the human nurse returned and was surprised how soundly the dwelf was sleeping, never even stirring while she used sponges and warm water to clean her up.

"You poor thing, you must have had a very traumatic experience. I only hope Doctor Nuria and Apothecary Maibrar don't make it any worse."

CHAPTER XXVII

NEW LIFE FROM THE EGG

"Full sail ahead to Jorvik!" shouted Asger, as he boarded the boat.

"Sire, is Ormr dead? And what is that egg?" the steersman of the ship asked.

"Ormr has died and will arise again, but we must hurry to Jorvik!" the warlock explained.

"Yes, Gothi Asger. You do recall we are quite far south of our home and it will take years to return, no?"

"I know, but just get us home as quickly as the sea will allow," he retorted.

"Yes, sire!"

Gothi Asger went to the bow of the ship and sat down with his legs crossed, placing the white egg with faint green spots in his lap. He then wrapped his arms around the egg as if he was embracing it with a hug.

Focusing on the figurehead of the ship, a fierce, white dragon, and he started to chant loudly,

"Ormr srow storr ok call,

Srow binn ess par til fallrinn.

Ase sem fastr sem madrr knatta,

Sva einn dasr bratt ver recurn til fit.

Sicyon munu fall hardr ok kaldr,

Sem varangianinn konungr tekr ahold!"

As he completed the magickal chant, he went into a trance while two amazing things simultaneously happened. The dragon figurehead of the ship began to slowly shrink while the egg in the warlock's lap started to vibrate and slowly grow.

The steersman, looking at the choppy seas ahead, walked back to the stern of the ship, looked at the skipari and quietly said, "I know the seas are going to be rough on the way back, but ol' crazy Asger wants us to hurry back with no delay."

The skipari stated, "I've seen him like this before. He will be in that trance for days. But be careful, he can hear anything that is said about him. When he wakes up, he will be in a very bad mood, especially if anything bad was said about him while he was in his trance."

"Thanks for the heads up," the steersman replied.

"Steersman, please take my post. I am going to have the journeyman cook prepare a meal for the holumenn, the styrimadr, the stafnbuaror sundvordr, and us."

"Skipari, I will let him know. Should he prepare a meal for Asger?"

"No, but when he comes out of that trance, there needs to be a meal and plenty of ale available for him. So, alert the journeyman cook about this as well. He needs to have a large amount of sustenance available for our Gothi the moment he awakes."

"I'll make sure he knows then. Let's get the boat moving!"

CHAPTER XXVIII

NO, NO, NOSKOMEIO

When Ti'erra started to wake up the next day, she was mumbling an odd chant,

"The purple dragon in the deep,

Healed me and put me to sleep.

She's been with me from the very start;

She lives with me, deep in my heart.

The goddess reveals herself slowly in time,

She'll save me from the approaching crime."

After chanting that, but being completely unaware of those actions, she gained her full consciousness again and was surprised to see that the doctor and apothecary were back in her room and had results.

"Ti'erra, we did not find anything out of the ordinary, but we would like to keep you here for observation for a few days," Doctor Nuria said.

"That is kind of you, but honestly, after the sleep, I feel completely better."

I don't think you understand. We aren't asking you. We are telling you!" Apothecary Maibrar stated with a devious tone in her voice.

Ti'erra got up and took off her gown, looking for her armour and greathammer.

Seeing it, she exclaimed, "No, I don't think you understand. I am a free woman, I have been kept without a free will as property in the past, and I will never let that happen again."

As she said this, the doctor and the apothecary walked towards her, where in the corner of her room, she was grabbing her armour.

"NOOOOOOOOOOOOOOOOOOOOOO! Get back, NOW!" she yelled, her voice echoing off the walls throughout the Noskomeio.

She knew she did not have time to get her giant tortoise armour on. So, she dropped it with a thud and reached for her greathammer's haft just as she heard a voice coming into her room from the hallway.

"Ladies, I believe the little lady said that she was leaving, and I suggest that you honour her wishes!" boomed the bold voice of Elder Dionysios.

The apothecary looked back and said, "Sir, you may have authority in your monasteries of The Way, but in this Noskomeio, you have no authority at all."

Elder Dionysios looked at them with seeming rage in his eyes, chanting as he stared down the two that would take his friend hostage, lifting the Budding Rod of Harun above his head and shaking it, saying, "The Ancient of Days hath converted my soul. He led me on the paths of righteousness of his name's sake. For even though I should walk in the midst of the shadow of death, yet I will not be afraid of evils; for thou art with me. Thy rod and thy staff..."

"Elder Dionysios, no!" screamed Doctor Nuria, "She is free to go. Please, no further escalation is necessary!"

He pointed his staff at the apothecary, and then, at the doctor and back to the apothecary, and said, "I think you should leave, NOW!"

"Yes, sir. Right away, sir!" said the apothecary as they scattered out of the room.

Ti'erra leapt into Elder Dionysios' arms and said, "Wizard, you saved me!" and kissed his cheek.

The Elder exhaled slowly and closed his eyes, saying, "It was nothing. You would have done the same thing, were our situations reversed. Now, please get dressed so we can leave."

He kept his eyes closed, and Ti'erra looked down and realised she was naked. '*No wonder the Elder had closed his eyes!*' she thought to herself, giggling. She went over and took her time, putting her armour on in a similar fashion of how she would take it off when dancing at The Pink Wyrm Tavern, just in reverse.

When she was done, Ti'erra said, "OK, Wizard, you can look now. Honestly, you could have looked the whole time."

Elder Dionysios looked at her big toothy smile and said, "You know I would never look upon you when you were not covered."

"I know, but I also wanted you to know that you could if you wanted to. You have my permission."

There was so much Dionysios could say to his friend, but he didn't want to sound nor be judgemental. So, he just sighed and carried her hammer as they exited the room and then, the Noskomeio itself.

"I have a bad feeling about this place, Wizard."

"I concur, Ti'erra. Something is not right here. We should keep our eyes and ears open about the goings-on about this place."

"Great idea. I will make sure I am being alert about what I hear at The Pink Wyrm Tavern."

"That is a great idea, Ti'erra. I am sure it is the hub of gossip and rumour."

"It definitely is, Wizard. Thanks again for saving me."

"It was my pleasure."

Elsewhere in the Noskomeio, Doctor Nuria and Apothecary Maibrar were talking about their failed attempt to get Ti'erra to stay.

"In the future, I think we need to use potions of unconsciousness and not depend on the non-human patients being willing to stay," the apothecary said.

"Sadly, we get so few non-human patients. So, I agree with you. We will just have to force the issue. Our experiments are far too important to the future of this world to allow free will to get in the way of our potential successes."

"I'm glad you finally agree with me, doctor. I only wish you had come to this conclusion earlier."

"I have to admit that you were right all along, Maibrar."

"Thank you, doctor. Sometimes, we need to break a few eggs to make an omelette."

The apothecary was glad that they were one step closer to their ultimate plans to create a new life that would be, in their estimation, the end of racial disharmony, wars, and death. Unfortunately, a few lives would have to end to make their dream a goal, but their sacrifices would be totally worth it. At least, that is what they thought and didn't care what anyone else said.

CHAPTER XXIX

CELEBRATING OUR HEROES

Lev Kakoi arranged Archon Justinian's Day of Sicyon's Heroes. It was not only an award ceremony for our heroes defeating the White Dragon but also a belated celebration of the Battle of Sicyon. During this time, Archon Justinian awarded three different awards after Lev introduced the archon of Sicyon.

"Ladies and Gentlemen, today, we gather at the centre of our fair city to award those, both human and non-human, that Archon Justinian has declared to be heroes of our fair and proud city of Sicyon. A city with centuries of a strong history where humankind has become the master of its own destiny. A city where every man and woman are a worthy individual.

In our history, our city has fought off all kinds of invasions from the worst of the evil beasts, grotesque goblins, horrible ogres, stupendous cyclopes, horrendous orcs, scary undead skeletons, devious dark elves, ghastly grey dwarves, and ferocious fey creatures. But until these 'heroes' banded together, we have never had to fight a diabolical dragon, a crazed cult, undead zombies, half-dragon, half-breed monsters, feral phoenixes, a dazzling drow priestess, a nasty necromancer, and even actual demons from the nine hells! No, we never were the focus of these types of attacks until these 'heroes' came to call Sicyon home. Thankfully, they were able to defeat them all, although at a great cost of life. So, before I introduce Archon Justinian, I would like us all to give a round of applause to our city guards who also fought against these monsters, and to then, bow our heads in silence for one full minute and remember those who have died in these horrible attacks on our 'heroes.'"

Lev then lowered his head and made a wicked smile. Archon Justinian was shocked at this introduction as it did explain why this group were worthy of the awards, it also hinted blame on them for the death and destruction that Sicyon had encountered at those attacks.

After one-minute, Lev continued, "So, it gives me great honour to introduce the head of the government of Sicyon, the man who has decided to today declare the ones in front of us to be the heroes of these recent attacks, Archon Justinian!"

Lev, along with all the townspeople started to clap in applause as their leader took stage front to announce the giving of awards.

The archon declared, "Without further ado, To Elder Dionysios, the Guardian of the Armour of the Ancient of Days... To Elder Mikhail, our dragon of the temple mount of Sicyon... To Archimandrite Miriam, the head of Sicyon's one and only Orphanage of the Transfiguration Cenobium that raises parentless children to be great citizens of Sicyon... and to Vhaidra, a dark elf who came to the surface and embraced all that is good in this land, this city, and in our people, the wife of the Chosen of The Ancient of Days... To these heroes, who have defended this city at great risk to their own lives, I bestow the *Taxi Prinkipa Ntaniel,* which is a symbol of The Way, four equal-sized circles in a larger circle, with a wreath around it which symbolises service."

Justinian hung the symbol over their necks with a solid blue strap.

Archon Justinian looked around in confusion, and then, asked Elder Dionysios, "Where is Skeletogre? He is supposed to be getting an award today too!"

Elder Dionysios walked over to Vhaidra and whispered in her ear. He then signalled over to the bag that he had brought with him on his staff. Vhaidra chanted to focus her qi and Skeletogre. The undead ogre rose from the bag, holding his twin scimitars with diamond blades and coral handles.

The crowd was shocked, seeing the giant undead creature's bones arise, ready to attack. Lev feigned like he was jumping in front of the archon to protect him but was really trying to fan the flames of panic and distrust.

Vhaidra shouted out, "Skeletogre, drop your weapons. Skeletogre, bow your head to the Archon."

———◆◆●◆◆———

"Doctor, Nurah, did you see that?" Apothecary Maibrar asked from amidst the stunned crowd.

"I sure did. That dark elf is much more than a simple monk."

"Don't you think that power would be helpful in our experiments?"

"I sure do. Do you think she will share her secrets with us, Maibrar?"

"Probably not."

"Well, then, we need to find a way to convince her to share her magicks with us."

"Agreed. I will leave that up to you, Maibrar."

"I won't fail you, Doctor Nurah. We will have her and her magicks in our grasp soon enough."

"Good. Now, let's mingle around in this crowd and look for other useful specimens as well."

"Aye," the apothecary replied, and they slowly started moving around, looking for those that they might find useful in their grand plans for Sicyon.

Skeletogre did as his mistress instructed him, and the archon went over and patted the giant undead creature's head in appreciation.

He then continued, "To Ti'erra, a former slave of the Jet Fist gang and a battle dancer whose tactics have helped our brave heroes defeat not only the Cult of the Jet Fist but also a White Dragon... Also, to Skeletogre, who acted as an extension of our dark elf heroine, slicing down so many zombies of the Jet First Cult during the Battle of Sicyon... To these heroes, I award the *Taxi Agiou Andrea*, a double-headed eagle emblem that symbolises duty to both our God and our land."

Justinian hung the symbol over both of their necks, on a yellow and black horizontally striped band. He had to stand on his toes to get the award over the enormous head of the undead ogre skeleton.

Archon Justinian completed the awarding of the symbols by saying, "Finally, to Hypodiakonos Nikodemos, a cleric of The Way and the Chosen of The Ancient of Days, who wears our God's armour on his very bones, the *Adelfotita Tis Agias Kyrias*, a star of one hundred points of light emanating from a small icon of The Ancient of Days. This signifies doing great service in the name of our God." Justinian hung the symbol over Nikodemos' neck with a light blue and white vertically striped strap.

"Please join me in a rousing round of applause for our heroes that we recognise today, in the Day of Sicyon's Heroes. To continue celebrating the day, we will have the Episkopos of our fair city lead a procession to the cemetery outside of town, where he will lead prayers for those who have died in the numerous battles that Sicyon has been part of over the last hundreds of years. The city will also declare today a tax-free day, where for this one day only, merchants do not need to collect taxes."

After the procession to the cemetery, the group retreated to the Iroas home, Omorfia Dipla Sto Potami, and found that a cake had been delivered, decorated with images of Nikodemos' Yan Yue Dao, Vhaidra's throwing daggers, Elder Dionysios' Rod of Harun, Ti'erra's greathammer, and Skeletogre's twin scimitars. There was orange frosting around the edges, which Mikhail decided would represent his fire breath weapon.

The heroes all enjoyed the cake, but not as much as the Iroas children, who loved sweets much more than the much older adults, even though they were considered to be or nearing the common age of adulthood for humans in Hellas.

The group stayed up, talking about the battles that earned them their awards, drinking wine, eating cake, and a meal that Vhaidra made in the evening.

―――•••●••••―――

The next day, all who partook of the cake found themselves mildly sick, except for Vhaidra, who was resistant to poison. Nikodemos mentioned that, perhaps, they should visit the Noskomeio, but Ti'erra, who had spent the night, said they absolutely should not, and instead, use healing potions, holy water, and their own natural medicines.

They did as the dwelf suggested, and within a day, were feeling better.

―――•••●••••―――

Unfortunately, they were never able to find out who had sent them the poisoned cake, nor were they able to find any reason that anyone in Sicyon should hate them. After all, they were just declared as the Heroes of Sicyon.

CHAPTER XXX

POWER, HATRED, LOVE, AND CONQUEST

"Mundi, what do your spies report?"

"Frea Jerrik, I have bad news to report."

"Please let us know."

"While we have had many successes along the path of lands to conquer, we have had a devastating setback at our final destination."

"In Sicyon, the small town in Hellas? How could a small town be problematic?"

"Well, sire, there appears to be a band of five adventurers that the village calls, 'The Heroes of Sicyon.'"

"Five adventurers, Mundi! What could they do against our Ormr?"

"Unfortunately, a lot, Frea Jerrik. They killed him."

"WHAT?" the king of the Varangians yelled in such a loud voice that it echoed through the entire council chambers, "How could five adventurers kill the last white dragon?"

"Sire, it is not completely clear right now, but it appears that they have their own dragons. I will be collecting more information, and now, I have an informer placed within a cult run by the town's second in command."

"The second in command runs a cult?"

"Yes, a very evil cult. They worship demons and sacrifice humans to these demons for power. The leader, a man named Lev, wants to take down these 'Heroes of Sicyon' and paint them as problematic for the village.

"Mundi, great thinking. I am still very upset that we have lost our greatest weapon that we have depended on for our successes. We are going to have to change our plans and throw all of our forces at Sicyon instead!"

As Frea Jerrik uttered these words, Queen Magnhild stood up next to her husband and calmly stated, "My Frea, we must have patience. We must listen to the prophecy. We must follow the 20-year plan as set-up by this council. We cannot be hasty and bring our doom from a group that killed our Ormr. No, we must take our time. After all, does the prophecy not say that it will be Frea Sigurd, not Frea Jerrik who will defeat the land of Hellas and that they will welcome him with open arms in the capital, Athinas? Surely, you do not plan to steal this honour from your son who has yet to be born?"

Tana the pixie floated up into the air and answered, "Queen Magnhild speaks the truth. Her words are bold but absolutely correct. Her words must have been spoken through her mouth by the Raven-Cloaked Goddess herself!"

Frea Jerrik looked at his wife, then at Tana, followed by Mundi, and the rest of the council, and sighed, "Your queen is completely correct. I am blessed to have both her and Tana advising this council. What say you, my council?"

Mundi raised his chalice and said, "Never has there been a fairer nor more intelligent queen in all of the Varangians than Queen Magnhild, who the goddess speaks through. Let us listen to her wise counsel and await the return of Gothi Asger and arrange our second of many attacks along the coasts of many lands then."

Slowly, one council member after another raised their chalices and shouted, "Aye."

Frea Jerrik looked to his wife and joked, "Are you trying to replace me with your wisdom, my wife? How can I compete with you, speaking the words of the goddess?"

"Oh, of course not, my Frea!" she gasped with a curtsey.

"To my wife, the wisest of wives, the future mother of Sigurd Jerrikson and the one who has spoken by the favour of the raven-cloaked goddess. We shall do as she has suggested."

"To the queen!" Tana shouted.

"To the queen!" everyone replied.

"Thank you, my Frea. Thank you my fellow Varangians. Your trust in my suggestions humbles me."

Tana whispered into Queen Magnhild's ear, and then, the queen stood up and asked to be excused to go get the meal for the council.

"You may not, my queen," Frea Jerrik replied, "The goddess spoke through you today, and so, you shall not serve but shall be served instead."

Frea Jerrik then turned to his council and said, "Who will serve the mouth of the Raven-Cloaked today?"

The men of the council all got up and rushed to the exit of the hall, and their king stopped them.

"Aye! It is good to see that you all wish to serve, but only one can have this honour, and in light of today's news, this honour falls to Mundi."

"Thank you, my Frea!" exclaimed the spymaster.

"Everyone else please be seated and await the meal that has been prepared for us."

When the meal did come in, Jerrik did something unusual and refused to let himself be served first. Instead, he said that his wife would be served first today and he was to be second.

Queen Magnhild was shocked and offered a toast to her husband, "To Frea Jerrik, the king of the prophecy, the Varangian who will set the path for the conquering of all the lands from here to Hellas!"

"To Frea Jerrik!" the council shouted in unison.

CHAPTER XXXI

A WHIMPER NOT A BANG

Within days, Damianos turned fourteen. With his parents' gleeful permission and blessings, he immediately joined the nearby boarding academy in Corinth to become a *paladin*. Paladins and paladins-in-training wore blue scale mail armour covered by silver-coloured plate mail that was supposed to mimic the original look of the golden Armour of The Ancient of Days, just in a different colour. They learned to use a matching great sword and a divine buckler strapped to their plate armour's left gauntlet. Strapping the very small buckler to the gauntlet allowed them to do two-handed attacks with their greatswords and still have some additional protection from attacks. Third-year paladins learned how to magickally change the divine shield from a tiny eight-inch diameter buckler to a large rectangular tower shield to protect themselves and others when the defence was more necessary than offence.

During his first year, Damianos quickly became friends with two of the other paladins, Xasha and Lio. Xasha was a common nickname for both the names of Alexander and Alexandra, while Lio was a nickname for Lionedas. Although his brother sometimes teasingly called him Dummy Dami, Damianos did not use a nickname and simply went by his name given to him by The Way, Damianos.

All three students were very successful in their studies and competed with each other for the highest scores in their training. While they all alternated in who scored the best, Xasha was the true shining star amongst them. Xasha just seemed to try even harder than the other assiduous students. They hoped that once they graduated, they would all be assigned to the same city together.

Although there was a statue of Hypodiakonos Nikodemos in the original form of the Armour of the Ancient of Days over his old red dragon scale armour at the front of the academy, Damianos did not tell people that he was the son of the chosen of their god, the Creator-Logos-Ghost, unless they were already aware of this fact. When they knew, he simply confirmed this fact and tried to quickly change the subject, wanting to be judged on his own merits, not those of his father.

Kosmas had long been enamoured in how to make beautiful weapons for himself, and so, that same year, even before he turned thirteen years old, he, with the blessings of his parents, became an apprentice in the local blacksmith shoppe run by TaeLyon, the duergar, the father of his best friend, Hemet the twin. TaeLyon required another apprentice with the increased demand of his wares, after becoming the official weapon and armour provider of the city of Sicyon.

Kosmas spent his free time with Hemet and his twin sister, Shelov, but did not actually have much free time at all, as he worked in the blacksmith shoppe with Hemet twelve hours a day as an apprentice to TaeLyon. Shelov spent that time learning baking, cooking, sewing, first aid, and also, fighting, so that she was a very effective fighter, possibly even more so than her twin brother, Hemet, who did not have as much time to train daily due to his full-time apprenticeship. Shelov helped out with apprentice work as well but focused more on work like sewing leather and dragon scale, as she was very good with this skill.

Hemet and Kosmas were so tight, tight as thieves, as they called it, that they took a blood oath. They promised to be best friends forever and to look after one another's family should anything happen to them. To seal this oath, they cut their palms and shook hands, bleeding into one another's wounds. This infuriated both sets of fathers, seeing it as an unnecessary injury that would make both of them less productive at work, but it also brought the two fathers, who were initially acquaintances, together, and they slowly started becoming friends.

Working in the blacksmith shoppe, Kosmas learned how he could use two perfectly balanced, dual-headed axes at the same time at a ferocious speed. He had preferred this type of weapon for many years, but now, realised how the perfect balance could enable him to attack even faster and with more fluidity. His favourite axes were the extremely shiny ones he helped TaeLyon create. It had a very detailed two-headed dragon design on each axe. While they were a very powerful and perfectly balanced weapon for dual wielding, they also were perfect for display as a beautiful piece of art.

Kosmas' best friend, Hemet, preferred twin double-headed war hammers, just like his twin sister, Shelov, did. This was probably because they were trained in their use since they were very young.

The twins had actually been trained for battle by their mother since their father was always busy in the forge. She had done so since they were two years old. As dwarven berserkers, in the heat of battle, they could go into an adrenaline-based rage that made them grow larger and fight fiercely, with no care to any possible injuries that they would take while on the offence. Their heavy plate armour was specially made to be able to expand with their size when they grew.

Unlike the human berserker, Odysseus, Nikodemos' deceased brother, these duergars could make smart tactical decisions when in their berserker state, due to years of mental, physical, and spiritual training. What they could not do, was make emotional decisions when in the berserker states. So, decisions were purely low-level logical ones.

YEAR 18

Almost a year later, when Athanasia was seventeen, she left her home to go on adventures and to explore the world. She travelled wearing black leathers, a black hooded velvet cape, with her urumi sword and scimitar hanging on her belt, as well as her poison-dipped dagger in hand. While her father initially objected to his daughter leaving on her own, Vhaidra finally convinced him that she was old enough, strong enough, and smart enough to be able to handle this responsibility. Vhaidra had taught her how to make deadly poison to coat the dagger, and one good slice from the poisoned blade would make any humanoid-sized creature die in a short time.

Athie left one calling crow with her family, in case she was ever needed in an emergency. Although Nikodemos was lacking belief, Athie assured her parents that the crow would know how to find her.

Unbeknownst to her parents, she had long been in contact with a mixed group of elves and half-elves via her calling crows for years, and during her recent journeys, she had come to live with this small group of various elven kind who were very unique in not seeing differences between the dark elves or drow, high elves, and wood elves or sylvan. They simply considered themselves to all be elves.

When she arrived at their home in a forest near Lechaeum, their tall leader, a full-blooded drow, grabbed Athanasia's hands, and looked at her, saying, "Priestess Quarae, we have awaited your arrival for seventeen years. Welcome to your destiny, sister!"

Athanasia responded, "I think you are confusing me with someone else, as I am no priestess, and my given name is Athanasia."

"Are you not the first daughter of Vhaidra of House Iroas, who we have been conversing with for years?" she asked Athanasia, scrunching up her nose.

"Yes, I am. But I am Athanasia, or Athie if you wish."

"You were, but now you are light, you are love, you are whole, you are blessed, you are legend, you are divine, you are the Priestess Quarae."

In this small society, all were seen as equals, except for the priestesses who reigned supreme, and all danced and sang together. This especially touched Athie as she had seen much racism against herself, the other half-humans, and other non-human races when she lived in Sicyon. She was quickly embraced by the group, and she embraced them as well, even if it was odd that their leader insisted on calling her 'Priestess Quarae.' Because of this, the others called her Quarae, her elven middle name, rather than her name given to her by The Way, Athanasia, or either of her nicknames that she was known by, Athie and Crow.

⸻ ••●•• ⸻

What Athanasia Quarae did not know was that each night Nikodemos had sent Mikhail, when doing his nightly flights, to fly out and follow her tracks, keeping an eye on her during her journeys. Once the half-dragon realised she was safe in a community of mostly female elves, he reported this back to Nikodemos and followed her no more.

EPILOGUE
THE FEY PLAGUE

YEAR 19

The worst was yet to come for *Vhaidra* and her friends. An illness had broken out in the underworld and overworld alike, sickening and killing elves of all types. *Dark elves, high elves,* and *wood elves* were all dying from this terrible disease. Had all of *Feykind* worked together, they may have found a solution to this sickness. Instead, the so-called *Fey Plague* or *Elven Pandemic* kept them isolated, and none of the fey communities tried to collaborate for a cure.

Eventually, it started to spread from the elven cities and communities to human cities. At first, it only affected elven kind, but eventually, *half-elves* also started to fall ill as well. But once the disease mutated and *humans* in *Sicyon,* as well as the rest of the world, started to get the sickness, it divided the city and much of the world into three very distinct camps.

The first group blamed all elves for this and wanted them banished from the towns and villages, and to ban any elves or half-elves from ever entering again.

The second group thought the disease was a conspiracy by the government officials to take away their rights by making them worry about elves and not corrupt government overreach.

The third group thought this was surely a sign of the last days and a soon-coming final judgement on all of creation.

⋯⋯●⋯⋯

While many religious people of *The Way* were in the third camp, *Archimandrite Miriam* of the *Transfiguration Cenobium and Orphanage* was in the first camp. She had all orphans that were not full-blooded humans moved to the orphanages of other cities and shut-down her monastery to anyone other than human followers of The Way, barring even the drow that she was nouna to, Vhaidra, and the half-dragon that she helped raise, *Mikhail.* While Elder Dionysios did not visit the cenobium anymore, if he had tried, he, too, would have been banned from entering under these strict new rules.

Mikhail smartly got around this by using his *dragon-borne* powers to assume the shape of a one hundred per cent pure human, reaching out to Archimandrite Miriam for spiritual advice. He felt bad deceiving her, but he saw her as almost a mother-figure and craved her spiritual teachings.

———••●••———

Vhaidra had long felt the hatred of her kind in the overworld from the first day she arrived from the underworld, and quickly, she found herself in the second camp, seeing this as just another plan of many racist humans in power using this illness to attack elves. *Elder Dionysios* did not disagree with her assessment of the situation. In fact, some hate-filled humans started posting signs offering rewards for bringing in the heads of any dead pointy-eared non-humans such as pixies, gnomes, elves, goblins, and orcs.

———••●••———

Hypodiakonos Nikodemos was in the last group and felt that if it was the end of the world, he was needing to be out in the world and saving people from the evil humans, beasts, and others that would surely be taking advantage of the situation. That could also possibly get his family away from the bad situation in Sicyon if they decided to do this as a mission trip away from their hometown. He also thought that this was likely everyone's last chance to get right with The Ancient of Days before the final judgement came. *Ti'erra*, although not a devout follower of The Way, tended to agree with him. Things definitely felt apocalyptic to her.

They would not get a chance to see if getting away would help, as the simple-minded beasts of the forests and lands just outside of Sicyon started noticing less human activity in the city along with fewer guards on watch due to quarantines. Wave by wave, these monstrosities would move in and try to take over the less secure city, as even in its plagued state had many valuable resources that these creatures would find useful. This was blamed on the elves by the first group.

While each group did have points that were, in fact, correct, they would all prove to be wrong. Deadly wrong. And for this, they would suffer greatly. However, one of the citizens of Sicyon took a different point of view. He was, perhaps, able to do this since he looked upon the city from a different place than anyone else. He did not live in a beautiful house at the city's walls, he did not live down in the catacombs below the city, nor did he live in a small home with other commoners. Instead, he lived on top of the temple mount. This was Mikhail the Obsidian Half-Dragon.

Mikhail took what he called the middle path and saw that yes, the disease did come from the elves, but it was not their fault that it spread to non-fey races. He also knew that being different caused attention, and for some that was fascination, for others it was hate of what they did not understand. He also considered that this might be the end times, but nothing that they did would change this if it was truly the will of The Ancient of Days. So, he perched upon the temple mount and prayed for all of the people of Sicyon, Hellas, and the whole world. Yet, he was prepared to fight and to defend all the people of Sicyon, no matter their opinion on this pandemic or him and other half-human or non-human races.

THE END
OF

VHAIDRA & THE DRAGON OF TEMPLE MOUNT

To be continued in the upcoming books:

Vhaidra & the DISEASE of Dark Elves

Vhaidra & the DESCENT of House Iroas

Vhaidra & the DEMISE of House Iroas

VHAIDRA & THE DUNGEONS OF DROW

VHAIDRA & THE DEMONS OF ZHONG

VHAIDRA & THE DIGEST OF SHORT STORIES

Vhaidra & the DELIVERANCE of Crow

Vhaidra & the DANCER of Darkness

Vhaidra & the DAUGHTERS of Deception

Vhaidra & the DEATH of Redacted

Vhaidra & the DENOUMENT of Everything

273

INDEX

SYNONYMS

- A *Wood Elf* is also called a *Sylvan*

- A *Dark Elf* is also called a *Drow*

- A *Grey Dwarf* or *Deep Dwarf* is also called a *Duergar*

- A *High Elf* is sometimes called an *Eladrin*

- A *Half-Elf* that is also a *Half-Dwarf* is called a *Dwelf*

- The *Spider Queen* is also known as the *Dark Mother*

- The *Dark Maiden* is also known as the *Dark Dancer*

- *The Ancient of Days* is also known as the *Creator-Logos-Ghost*

INDEX

NICKNAMES

- Vhaidra always calls Hypodiakonos Nikodemos, *"Hypo"*

- Ti'erra always calls Hypodiakonos Nikodemos, *"Cleric"*

- Ti'erra always calls Vhaidra, *"Monk"*

- Ti'erra always calls Elder Dionysios, *"Wizard"*

- Ti'erra calls Miriam, *"Milkmaid"* at first and then later, *"Ranger"*

- Nikodemos' friends call him, *"Demos"*

- Athanasia is also known as *"Crow," "Athie,"* and *"Quarae"*

INDEX

Etymology of Fantasy Races

- *Brain Floggers* were psionic creatures that have eight tentacles in place of their lips and nose that are actually two creatures in a symbiotic relationship. Their design and powers were fashioned after the early twentieth-century monster deity, *Cthulhu.*

- *Bugbears* is a word in use since at least the sixteenth-century A.D. and originates from the German word *Bogge,* the Old Scots word *Bogill,* the Old Welsh word *Bwg,* and the Middle English word *Bugge.* They are usually described as large, hairy *Hobgoblins,* which are larger, smarter *Goblinoids.*

- *Bulettes* is another name for a *Land Sharks* and first gained popularity in Japanese monster movies and Hong Kong toy sets in the mid-twentieth-century before being used in the role-playing game *Chainmail.*

- *Cyclopes* were one-eyed giant monsters found in writing as far back as the sixth century B.C. and comes from the Greek *Kyklops*.

- *Dark Elves* comes from the Old Norse word *Dokkalfar*. *Dark Elves* are also known as *Drow*. *Drow* comes from the Scottish word *Trow*. These terms are found being used as far back as the thirteenth century A.D. They have dark grey skin, white hair, and their eyes have been known to range from yellow to green or red to purple.

- *Dragons* comes from the Ancient Greek *Drakon* and the creatures have been mentioned as far back as the twenty-first century B.C. They are colourful giant lizards that can fly. In the west they have wings, in the east, they do not and fly by magickal force of will. They often can take the shape of another creature, often humanoids, by use of their powerful magicks.

- *Dwarves* comes Old High German *Twerg* and Proto-Germanic *Dwergaz* and has been in use since at least the thirteenth century. Sub-races include *Hill* or *Gold Dwarves* and *Grey Dwarves* or *Duergars*. They tend to be short and stout. Males often go bald and start growing a beard during adolescence.

- *Elementals* are mythic beings of air, earth, fire, and water of various sizes that have been found in writing as far back as the sixteenth-century A.D.

- *Elves* comes from the Old English *Aelf* and Germanic *Alfr*. The terms are found being used as far back as the tenth century A.D. Their race is also known as *Fey* or *Feykind*. Sub-races include *Dark Elves or Drow, High Elves or Eladrin,* and *Wood Elves or Sylvan*. They are usually shorter than humans, thin, beautiful, and quick. They are famously known for their long, pointed ears.

- *Giants* comes from the Greek word *Gigantes* and was in use as early as the thirteenth century A.D. but is also related to the Old Norse word *Jotunn* and the Hebrew *Nephilim* from the *Torah* portion of the *Old Testament* of the Jewish and Christian *Bibles*. These creatures often look like humanoids but are much larger.

- *Goblins* was used as early as the twelfth century A.D. in various languages as *Gobelin* in Old

French, *Kobalos* in Greek, and *Gobelinus* in Latin. A *Hobgoblin* is a larger or rustic version of the creature. They are short and thin with green to yellow colour skin.

- *Grey Dwarves* or *Deep Dwarves* comes from the Old Norse word *Svartalfar*. *Grey Dwarves* are also known as *Duergars*. *Duergars* comes from the Old Norse word *Dvergar*. These terms are found being used as far back as the thirteenth century A.D. They are short, stout, and have medium to dark grey skin and white hair. Males go bald and start growing a beard during early adolescence.

- *High Elves*, *Light Elves*, and *Sun Elves* all come from the Norse word *Ljosalfar*. The usage of this terminology is found being used as far back in the thirteenth century A.D. They have extremely pale skin, hair, and eye colours; however, some rare exceptions have been known to have black or other colours of hair.

- *Kobolds* is thought to come from the German word *Galgenmannlein* even though it is similar to the Greek word for goblins. The word has been in use since at least the thirteenth century

A.D. They are often described as enemies of goblins that look like small, usually red, draconic humanoids not unlike a half-dragon.

- *Liches* is an Old English word for *Corpse* and was used as far back as the eleventh century A.D., if not earlier but became a term for an undead monster in the early twentieth-century A.D. Undead monsters were once dead, but brough back to unlife through powerful magicks.

- *Lycanthropes* comes from the Greek word, *Lukanthropos,* and has been in use since at least the fifth century B.C. Today most people call them *werewolves, werebears, wererats,* and *werebats.*

- *Manticores* comes from the Early Middle Persian *Merthykhuwar* and has been used as early as the fifth century B.C. and is similar to the Egyptian *Sphinx.*

- *Ogre* and *Ogress* are French words originating from the Latin *Orcus* and was used as early as the twelfth century A.D. They are huge creatures with large heads and often have yellowed skin.

- *Orcs* comes from the Latin *Orcus,* and was used as early as the eleventh century A.D. They are larger than humans, very muscular and tend to have a green to grey skin colour. They have been known to mate with humans, creating *Half-Orcs*.

- *Owlbears* first gained popularity in Japanese monster movies and Hong Kong toy sets in the mid-twentieth-century A.D. before being used in the role-playing game *Chainmail. They look much like a bear with a bird of prey's head, sometimes owl-like, sometimes not.*

- *Oozes,* the most famous of which is the *Gelatinous Cube* were first found used as a monster in the middle twentieth-century A.D., first with the movie *The Blob.* Just like gelatin, they can come in many shapes and sizes.

- *Rothe* are furry black herd mammals exactly like overworld yaks that live in the underworld. They were likely first used in the late twentieth-century A.D. in many role-playing games such as *Dungeons & Dragons.*

- *Rust Monsters* first gained popularity in Japanese monster movies and Hong Kong toy sets in the middle to late-twentieth-century A.D. before being used in the role-playing game *Chainmail.*

They look somewhat like a giant termite that eats metal instead of wood.

- *Succubi* is a Middle English word that comes from the Latin word *Succubae,* it can be found in use since the eleventh century A.D. They are demons that feed on a male's soul during copulation.

- *Troglodytes* comes from the Greek word, *Trogle,* it can be found being used as far back as the fifth century B.C. They are a primitive cave-dwelling reptilian humanoid creature.

- *Vampires* comes from the twelfth century A.D. word *Vampyrs* and is prevalent on both western and eastern European culture as well as on the Indian sub-continent. They have long fangs and sustain themselves on the blood of others.

- *Wood Elves,* the fey subrace of many fairy tales were first called *Silvan* and later *Sylvan* in Early Modern English. They tend to have red or brown hair and a golden tan to brown skin colour.

INDEX

Names & Meanings

- *Alakzar* (Best Mate) *of House Oussviir* (Heirs to Dominance)

- *Alaunual* (Lightning Speed) *the Archimandrite of Hun'rahel* (Sisterhood of the Goddess) *Cenobium*

- *Athanasia* (Eternal Life) *'Crow' Quarae* (Eternal Life) *of House Iroas*

- *Aunyl* (Dead Drow) *of House of Godeep* (Clan of the Underworld)

- *Barachial* (Lightning of God) *Altonerd* (Lightning God)

- *Brizinil* (Graceful Lady) *Vhaidra's mother of House Oussviir* (Heirs to Dominance)

- *Charissa* (Kind and Gracious)

- *Damianos* (To Tame) *Elkaugh* (Chaos Breaker) *of House Iroas*

- *Dionysios* (Belonging to the Light of the Tree)

- *Eskandar* (Defender of Man)

- *Feyrdryl* (Dark Dancer)

- *Gunhild* (Battle in a War)

- *Halisstra* (Deft Acolyte) *the Archimandrite of Yochlol* (Handmaiden of the Spider Queen) *Lavra*

- *Helena* (Bright, Shining Light) *the nouna of Athanasia*

- *Hemet* (Master of Destiny) *Axenforge* (Makes Perfect Axes)

- *Ilphe* (Emerald Servant) *the Archimandrite of Xunquarra* (Demon Horde) *Skete*

- *Irriina* (Hidden Enchanter) *of House Tekken'duis* (Delvers in the Whip)

- *Jerrik* (King Forever)

- *Justinian* (Righteous, Upright)

- *Kosmas* (Beautiful Order) *Masvayas* (Beauty Forger) *of House Iroas*

- *Larzyr'ss* (Lawful Sage Scout)

- *Leib* (Little Lion)

- *Lev* (Lionheart) *Kakoi* (Son of Belial)

- *Lionedas* (Like a Lion) *Kaiser* (Emperor)

- *Magnhild* (Powerful in Battle)

- *Maibrar* (Death crafter)

- *Mikhail* (Gift from God)

- *Miriam* (Sea of Bitterness and Sorrow) *Mosseri* (Of Misr)

- *Myronia* (Lost Staff), *Monk of Xunquarra* (Demon Horde) Skete

- *Nikodemos* (Victory of the People) *Iroas* (Chosen Hero)

- *Nurah* (Hopeful beast)

- *Odysseus* (To Hate)

- *Rokmaw* (Strength of the Mountains)

- *Romanos* (Strong & Powerful) *Rousopoulos* (Descendants from Rus')

- *Sophia* (Wisdom) *Sarras* (Fair Headed)

- *Shelov* (Healer) *Axenforge* (Makes Perfect Axes)

- *Sigurd* (Victory Warrior) *Jerrikson* (Son of The King Forever)

INDEX

HEROES & TREASURES: ICE & FLAME

Vhaidra and Hypodiakonos Nikodemos appear in the upcoming *Heroes & Treasure* Expansion Game, *Heroes & Treasure: Ice & Flame,* an original fantasy role-playing game for the whole family by Davis & Daughters Games! Order your copy of the original and all of the exciting expansion games today at *http://HeroesAndTreasure.com* and have your chance to have an interactive, never-before told adventure, with both Vhaidra the dark elf monk and Nikodemos the human cleric, during their exciting first year exploring the overworld together, taking place between the pages of *Vhaidra & the DESTINY of Nikodemos.* The artwork behind this text is the actual art of Vhaidra the dark elf monk used to create her *Heroes & Treasure* miniature, which is included in the expansion game, *Heroes & Treasure: Ice & Flame.*

INDEX

NOVELS OF THE VHAIDRA SAGA

I: Vhaidra & the DESTINY of Nikodemos Published in 2020. The *Cult of the Jet Fist* literally causes the forces of heaven and hell to collide, destroying *Sicyon* in the process. Meanwhile, the *Dark Maiden* starts drawing a line of destiny from the past to the future, intersecting with the lifelines of Vhaidra and *Nikodemos,* as one house dies, and another is formed. The stand-alone novel that starts the ever-expansive chronicles of Vhaidra and House Iroas.

II: Vhaidra & the DRAGON of Temple Mount Published in 2021. The war of the Dragons begins here. House Iroas ascends as *Vhaidra* and *Hypo* raise a powerful house of half-drow warriors in the overworld. Meanwhile, the orphaned young half-dragon, *Mikhail,* his human milkmaid & astonishing ranger, *Miriam,* and the flirtatious dwelf dancer, *Ti'erra,* change the ascetic half-orc hermit, *Elder Dionysios,* forever, whether he likes it or not. The obsidian half-dragon grows from a baby to *Sicyon's* powerful stylite and protector after the earth-shattering events of *VHAIDRA & the DESTINY of NIKODEMOS* and leading into the cataclysmic events of *VHAIDRA & the DISEASE of DARK ELVES.*

III: Vhaidra & the DISEASE of Dark Elves Publishing soon. Shortly after the life-changing events of VHAIDRA & the DRAGON of TEMPLE MOUNT, an epidemic starts to spread across Hellas from the elven lands. As it eventually becomes a pandemic, it divides the city and our adventurers into three very different camps; one group blames all elves—high, wood, and dark—for the pandemic and starts persecuting them, another thinks it is a false flag conspiracy by the government to separate them into groups to more easily control them, and the last camp is scared to death, thinking it is a sign of it being the last days. Whomever is right, the beginning of a deadly zombie apocalypse is upon them and there is no more time to argue, only a need to act!

IV: Vhaidra & the DESCENT of House Iroas Publishing soon. After the cataclysmic events of VHAIDRA & the DISEASE of DARK ELVES, Vhaidra learns the whereabouts of the last remaining survivors of her house from the underworld, just as her cold dish of revenge is finally ready to be served, but at what cost? Death finally claims many of our heroes' lives while House Iroas changes the underworld forever. To be concluded in VHAIDRA & the DEMISE of HOUSE IROAS.

V: Vhaidra & the DEMISE of House Iroas Publishing soon. A direct continuation of the story from VHAIDRA & the DESCENT of HOUSE IROAS. Stuck in the deepest depths of the underworld with half of our heroes now dead, will the one true chosen one rise from the ashes of the battle with the Spider Queen and save the overworld from certain destruction from below? No one comes out unscathed and no one will ever look at what remains of House Iroas the same way ever again!

VI: Vhaidra & the DUNGEONS of Drow Publishing soon. What strange secrets does Vhaidra's long-lost indestructible staff hold and how is it connected to the goddess known as the Spider Queen? This is the in-depth untold story of Vhaidra's conception, birth, and life in the cities and monasteries of the underworld of the evil Dark Mother, as told by Vhaidra to a familiar messenger crow belonging the demi-goddess Alkonost following the emotionally scarring events of VHAIDRA & the DEMISE of HOUSE IROAS. Characters and events from this story of Nikodemos' past will take centre stage in his not-so distant future.

VII: Vhaidra & the DEMONS of Zhong Publishing soon. The untold in-depth story of Nikodemos and his introduction to the Armour of the Ancient of Days by Presbyteros Romanos, as told to Vhaidra after the shocking events of VHAIDRA & the DEMISE of HOUSE IROAS. We learn what really happened when the hypodiakonos first encountered the six succubi during his journeys to the mysterious lands of the far east, the dire warning that he receives, and the item that he obtains which will change his destiny forever! Characters and events from this story of Nikodemos' past will take centre stage in his not-so distant future.

VIII: Vhaidra & the DAMNED of Hellas Publishing soon. Drow, dwarves, gnomes, and humans from Vhaidra's and Nikodemos' past come to a collision course in Sicyon when a vampire arises from the underworld that has a connection to Vhaidra. This forces Miriam and Vhaidra to team up in striking out to stop not only the ever-increasing number of vampires, but the perception that Vhaidra, as Sicyon's first Drow resident, is to blame. And what connection do these vampires have with the lycanthropes that have started to appear in Sicyon? Just when they think everything is over, a second waves hits and is concluded in VHAIDRA & the DOCTOR of ABOMINATIONS!

IX: Vhaidra & the DOCTOR of Abominations Publishing soon. Erupting from the pages of VHAIDRA & the DAMNED of HELLAS, The

Noskomeio has many strange things coming from it, which brings the attention of SNEZHANA the half-orc Barbarian as well as BERILANI the gnome warlock, and her band of wolves, who are looking for the source of the lycanthropes plaguing Hellas. But lycanthropes are not the only thing haunting the region. While the Noskomeio's doctor and the apothecary may only have good intentions, their experiments bring unnatural terrors upon VHAIDDRA, NIKODEMOS, TI'ERRA, MIKHIAL, and the other residents of Sicyon. It is all-out monster mayhem in the city of abominations as SKELETOGRE meets his final destiny as the doctor and apothecary make a final stand against the war between the various races of the world.

X: Vhaidra & the DIGEST of Short Stories Publishing soon, not a digest on stand-alone stories of the early lives of Dogork the Ogre that become Skeletogre, Ulviirae the half-sister of Vhaidra, Imfein the Drow Bard, Ti'erra's mother, potential fathers, and the war that the brought them together, Elder Dionysios, and finally the true hidden story of the Doppelgangers, including Mikhail's mother, Feyrdryl, the Obsidian Dragon! Find out the secret stories behind the hidden mysteries of the friends and family of Vhaidra the dark elf monk.

INDEX

ABOUT THE AUTHOR

*N*icholas *Stanosheck*, besides being an author, is a father, a world traveller, a volunteer Scout Leader, an Orthodox Christian, and a Lean Six Sigma Master Black Belt from Lincoln, Nebraska, USA who currently resides in Dallas, Texas, USA. His novels come from his lifelong love of fantasy novels, video games, world travels, and role-playing games. His first novel started as a short story that he had in his head for years, and once he committed it to writing, the characters spoke to him and started telling him a series of stories about *THE VHADRA SAGA* that will continue as a paperback and e-book series for years to come. You may contact him at http:// Vhaidra.com.

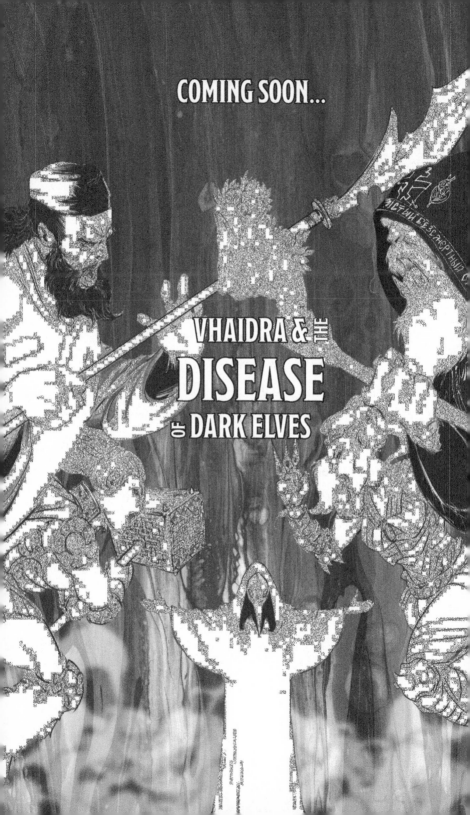

Made in the USA
Monee, IL
19 March 2021